HOOPERS

Johnny Boateng

James Lorimer & Company Ltd., Publishers
Toronto

James Lorimer & Company Ltd., Publishers acknowledges funding support from
the Ontario Arts Council (OAC), an agency of the Government of Ontario.
We acknowledge the support of the Canada Council for the Arts, which
last year invested $153 million to bring the arts to Canadians throughout the
country. This project has been made possible in part by the Government of
Canada and with the support of Ontario Creates.

Cover design: Tyler Cleroux
Cover image: AdobeStock

Library and Archives Canada Cataloguing in Publication (Paperback)

Title: Hoopers / Johnny Boateng.
Names: Boateng, Johnny, author.
Series: Sports stories.
Description: Series statement: Sports stories
Identifiers: Canadiana (print) 20210201436 | Canadiana (ebook) 20210201444
    | ISBN 9781459416352 (softcover) | ISBN 9781459416369 (EPUB)
Classification: LCC PS8603.O23 H66 2021 | DDC jC813/.6—dc23

Published by:
James Lorimer &
Company Ltd., Publishers
117 Peter Street, Suite 304
Toronto, ON, Canada
M5V 0M3
www.lorimer.ca

Distributed in Canada by:
Formac Lorimer Books
5502 Atlantic Street
Halifax, NS, Canada
B3H 1G4

Distributed in the US by:
Lerner Publisher Services
241 1st Ave. N.
Minneapolis, MN, USA
55401
www.lernerbooks.com

Printed and bound in Canada
Manufactured by Friesens Corporation in Altona, Manitoba,
Canada in June 2021.
Job #277240

Dedicated to the SQUAD, my guy Ving Rhames and all my Evansville, SFU and JL Crowe hoopers. T-Bo, Dru, Rosco, LP, Coledi, JA, Lank, BSizzle, Chrizzle, Emdre and Big Kwams the legend — we brothers for life.

Contents

1 For the CULTURE

Hip hop music blasts from a wireless speaker box. On the court, three Grade Nine boys dance as they dribble basketballs in figure eights between their legs.

"Aye! Aye! Aye!" the boys shout as they do the Milly Rock dance.

Jojo Antwi loves hanging out at the basketball court with his two best friends, Jose Santos and Brendo McMahon. They are there all the time, even when they aren't playing basketball.

Jose and Brendo take a break and cool off on the bench. But Jojo keeps dribbling the basketball in and out of his legs.

"I can't wait for these tryouts, bro," says Jojo with a slight West African accent.

"Man, we're going to put the Westwood Squad back on the map." Jose says.

"I heard there's a new coach." Brendo says.

"Don't matter. I'm finna kill at will, all I need is the pill." Jojo smiles and nods. The look on his face says, *let's do this*.

As Brendo and Jose jump to their feet, Jose positions his phone on the bench and pushes record.

"Let's get it!" Jojo shouts.

Ball under his arm, Jojo paces back and forth on his long legs. He looks like a prize fighter ready to step into the ring. Brendo, a lanky white boy with long, curly black hair, claps his hands and steps in front of Jojo.

"Me first," Brendo says. "Uh, uh, yo check it — I got handles, wax your ankles to shambles, my game on and popping like roman candles. Call me Boom, but my birth cert say Brendo, no new friends yo, big baller like Lonzo, hooper till the end yo."

"Yo, yo, yo," Jojo starts.

"Spit Jo!" Brendo shouts.

"Yo, yo, I do it for the culture. I spit that heat, I'm elite, haters I eat, and leave them scraps for the vultures."

"Okay, okay!" Brendo shouts.

Jojo continues to freestyle. "I break ankles, then make it rain. I drop bombs on your moms with no shame, hit you with that two and three like I'm King James. Destined for fame, king of the black top, Jesus Shuttlesworth, he got game."

Jose's curly brown afro bounces as he starts dancing. His small, wiry frame deftly executes cool dance moves as he starts his freestyle. "Ima true hooper, I got the scoop for the pooper, Paul Pierce the truth uh. I'm cold straight snatch your soul, overlooked like D Book, but I still drop dimes in between the lines."

The boys cheer each other and give each other high-fives.

"Straight bars," Brendo says.

"Boss flex," Jojo agrees. "Except Jose, did you say you had the scoop for the pooper? What the hell, brethren?"

"It was fire, right? Don't be capping." Jose smiles, retrieving his phone.

"You right gang, sounded cool AF." Jojo laughs.

"My flow just hit different!" Jose declares as he replays the song on his phone.

Jojo dribbles the basketball. "Chill, chill, chill," he stutters like a semi-automatic. "Let's hoop some more."

"Seriously, bro?" Brendo says.

"Let's go play some 2K," Jose suggests.

"Wait, bro," says Brendo. "Can you actually improve your game in real life playing 2K?"

"Oh my, seriously, bro? It's totally obvious. I can't believe you didn't know that."

"That's actually smart. Working on that basketball IQ. I see you, baby. Respect," Brendo says.

Jose points to his head, like he's a mastermind. Jojo rolls his eyes, he thinks it's nonsense.

"Guard me for a hot sec," Jojo says.

Brendo steps forward. "Check up."

Jojo checks the ball.

"Shoot, I'll you give that."

Jojo hoists up a shot. Brendo jumps and just barely grazes Jojo's hand as he releases the ball. The ball sails wide left, an air ball.

"Foul," Jojo calls.

"Wow," retorts Brendo. "You can't be serious."

"Bro, you hit me."

"Hell, no."

"Respect the call, bro."

"Jojo, that is so soft."

"Yo, Jose, he fouled me, right?" Jojo's voice raises as he appeals to Jose.

Jose shakes his head. "That's cap!"

"No cap. Don't do me like this, Jose," Jojo pleads.

"Fine," Jose says. "I didn't see it."

"See? Respect the call."

"Weak sauce, Jose," Brendo says as he retrieves the ball. "Check ball!" Brendo angrily throws the ball back at Jojo.

Jojo drives the ball and dips his shoulder into Brendo's chest. Then he lays the ball into the hoop. "And — oooooooooooone!" Jojo yells at the top of his lungs.

Jose grabs the ball. "I got him. Check ball." He crouches into a defensive stance.

Jojo starts his move with an in-between crossover, and then he shifts his body weight.

Then Jojo crosses and drives past Jose to the hoop.

Jose gives chase, but he's too late. He gives a last reach at Jojo's arm as Jojo goes to the hoop for a lefty layup.

But Jojo misses. The ball spins in and out of the hoop.

Jose snatches the rebound. "Oh! He blew it!"

"And one!" Jojo yells.

Both Jose and Brendo groan in unison.

"Hell, no!" Jose shouts.

"This guy calls foul on every freakin' play when he misses," crows Jose.

"Ya'll don't play any D, man. Hacking the crap out of me!" Jojo shouts.

"Nah, shoot for it then," Jose counters.

Brendo makes a confused face. "Shoot for it? But he —"

"Okay!" breaks in Jojo. "I will shoot for it. Give me the rock!"

Jojo spins the ball in his hands and hoists up a shot. The ball ricochets violently off the side of the rim, missing badly.

"Ball don't lie!" Brendo shouts.

Jojo grabs his own shoulder. "Yo, that didn't feel right. My shoulder is tired or something."

Jose retrieves the ball. "Yo check it, my ball."

"Nah, I'm done." Jojo says, walking away.

"That's messed up, Jojo."

Suddenly breathing heavily, Jojo grabs a water bottle. "I'm gassed, bro."

"We only played a couple possessions."

"I'm cashed. Let's call it."

"It was your idea to run kings!" Brendo shouts.

"I thought I had it in me," Jojo says. "But I'm done. My bad."

"You just don't want to get that work from me," Jose mutters.

"Whatever. Here, get me." Jojo hands his phone to Brendo. "How many should I do?"

"How many can you do in thirty seconds?" Brendo asks.

"I'll just do like ten or so, then you can stop filming. But don't come in till I've done a couple first."

"Aight."

Brendo films while Jojo does his push-ups. Jojo grunts on the last one and pops to his feet, like he's just done a hundred. Then he grabs his phone from Brendo. He posts the video with the hashtags #grinding, #Squad and #ballislife.

A few seconds later, the phone starts buzzing and doesn't stop. Jojo smiles to himself, knowing the sound of likes. He looks and sees that there are comments too.

But there is one comment that stands out: *You ain't #Squad yet.*

Jojo doesn't recognize the user. "Trolls," he mutters.

2 Making the SQUAD

Jojo, Jose and Brendo walk through the streets of North York together, laughing and joking with each other. They strut into the Westwood gym wearing matching shorts.

Jojo feels his crew has street credit with the other basketball players. Earlier that summer, the trio finished fourth place in a three-on-three tournament in Markham. Jojo's 'Gram post about the win got them mad respect and a small following.

Jojo looks around the gym at all the players there for the tryout and smirks. "BBQ chicken tonight!" he shouts.

Jojo heard people say that he didn't dribble well. That he couldn't really shoot. That it looked like he was out of shape. To him, it was all trolls and haters. As far as Jojo was concerned, he was a hooper. He was going D1, the highest level of play, and no one could tell him otherwise.

Three East Indian eleventh graders named Harmon,

Ram and Jazz walk in after Jojo and his friends, wearing Squad team shorts. They're returning players.

"Nice shorts," Jazz says, laughing at them.

Jojo, Jose and Brendo stare them down with mean mugs.

"You still salty?" Jojo asks. The three-on-three was so competitive, there is still some bad blood between the two crews.

Tweet! A single whistle blast rings so loud and with so much force, it startles the entire gym full of boys into attention.

A stocky Black man in his mid-thirties jogs into the gym. He's in great shape, with big arms and a barrel chest. He wears a tight black T-shirt with SQUAD written across the front and he carries himself with astute posture.

"Bring it in!" the coach barks.

Jojo can feel the force of the bass in the coach's voice. The longer he looks at the coach, the more he begins to feel intimidated.

"I'm tripping." Jojo says to himself, trying to shake it.

At the back of the gym, a red-haired boy, wearing a Morris Peterson jersey, black corduroy pants and black dress shoes, doesn't stop at the whistle and keeps shooting.

The coach snaps his head around. "Hey!" he shouts as he marches towards the kid.

Running full speed towards the hoop, the kid

attempts a double-clutch layup. The point-blank shot sails wildly over the backboard. He turns around to find the coach inches away from his face.

Brendo and Jose struggle to keep straight faces. Jojo holds the ball up in front of his face to hide his smile. He glances at Jose and Brendo and has to turn away. Just looking at them makes him want to burst out in laughter.

"Didn't you hear the whistle?" the coach asks the kid.

"Yes," the kid responds.

"Oh, you did?" The coach doesn't break eye contact.

"Yes."

"And did you not see that everyone else stopped shooting?" His voice is raised.

The kid goes silent. He's clueless.

The coach looks him up and down. Then he says, "You're cut. Thank you for coming out. Dress appropriately next time. Goodbye."

Then the coach turns his attention to the rest of the players. "My name is Coach Pritchard; I'm the new coach here at Westwood. Welcome to the tryouts for the Westwood Central Squadron varsity team. If you do not perform well, you will be cut. If you fool around, you will be cut. If you stop listening, or I have to compete for your attention . . . cut. Are we clear?"

All the boys nod.

"If we're clear, acknowledge your understanding by saying, *Yes, Coach*."

"Yes, Coach!" Jojo and the rest of the boys shout.

"Okay! Balls away. Everyone on the baseline!"

Balls away? Jojo thinks. Isn't this a basketball tryout? He and the rest of the boys walk towards the baseline.

"Hold on," says Coach Pritchard.

They all stop.

"I told you to get to the baseline. And now we're walking? At a tryout? Not one of you ran. I guess we need to learn how to hustle."

Twenty-nine minutes later, the boys are still running lines. Jojo is done. He's had it. Were they going to run lines for the whole tryout?

"Ridiculous," Jojo says under his breath. "This is some bull," he whispers as he cruises back to the baseline.

"Young man."

Jojo turns to see Coach Pritchard staring at him.

"Young man, why aren't you running hard?"

Jojo can feel his heart racing. He's scared of being caught and it's hard to speak.

"I — I," he stammers.

"Do you think you're better than everyone else?" Coach Pritchard asks.

Jojo's mind goes blank.

"What is your name, big fella?"

"Jojo."

"That's your full name?" Coach Pritchard asks.

"Jojo Antwi."

"Jojo Antwi, why aren't you running hard?"

"I was tired," Jojo says.

"We haven't been running for thirty minutes and already you're ready to quit?"

"No, Coach, I'm not quitting."

Coach Pritchard turns to the rest of the boys. "Thanks to Jojo, you now have five more lines. Consequences, gentlemen."

After the lines and a short water break, Coach finally allows the boys to pick up the basketballs.

Jose and Brendo run over to Jojo.

"Yo, what was that?" Jose whispers.

"Who is this guy?" Brendo whispers.

"He talking crazy," Jojo says.

Jojo dribbles the ball between his legs and hoists a deep fadeaway three-pointer.

The ball ricochets off the rim, wide left.

Coach Pritchard starts marching over, but Jojo is looking at the basket. Jose and Brendo try to get Jojo's attention.

"Feels right coming off my hand," Jojo says to his friends. "I have that, just need to get warm again, y'all know."

"Is that the shot you're going to take in a game?" Coach Pritchard snaps.

Jojo whips around. "Uh —"

"Do you practice taking that shot?"

"Uh — I mean, yes."

"You do?"

"Yeah. I mean, I do sometimes."

"How many shots do you shoot per day?" Coach Pritchard asks.

"Per day?" Jojo asks.

"Start closer to the basket. And try mastering mid-range fundamental jumpers, first."

Jojo thinks the way Coach says "start closer to the basket" is a diss. *He doesn't think I have this,* Jojo thinks to himself. *And he's calling me out in front of everyone, again.*

Coach Pritchard calls for the boys to break up and play king of the court.

A little angry and full of aggression, Jojo drives it hard to the hoop. He scores with a power-move layup. The biggest guy in his group, Jojo starts throwing his body into the other boys, playing bully ball. Jojo scores in all sorts of different ways. Jojo dominates his hoop to the point where he feels he has to start talking.

"Yo, I'm killing ya'll," Jojo says.

"No flex, dude. We're just here to have fun," a kid in a blue headband says.

"Hold this three for fun," Jojo says. He hoists up a deep three-pointer. The ball banks off the backboard and drops in.

"You didn't even call bank," complains the kid.

Jojo leaves his hand up. "I called game!"

Jojo checks to see if Coach Pritchard has seen him dominate. But he can see no reaction.

★★★

After the tryout, Jojo, Jose and Brendo are the last to leave the locker room.

"Yo, man, that was tough," Brendo says.

"Just imagine what practice is going to be like," Jose says. Then he adds, "at least we weren't Jojo today."

Brendo and Jose laugh.

"Yo this guy, Coach," Jojo says. "Man, he was cheesing me right?"

"Yeah, bro," his friends agree.

Jojo doesn't like the vibe that he's getting from Coach Pritchard. All he knows is that Coach has something against him, something personal.

3 Shoot Your SHOT

"That's the block party, right there," Jose says excitedly. "That house right there."

Jojo takes a selfie. He posts, "We pulled up, Party hype AF #squad" to his Instagram page.

Right behind him, Jose snaps a selfie of himself.

The house on the corner has kids piling in and out of it. Jojo can see the basketball courts in the park across the street are also filled with partying kids.

"Oh, this is lit," he says.

The two boys enter the house party to be greeted by a giddy Brendo. He can't seem to wipe the smile from his face.

"What's good, Brendo?" Jojo asks.

"Bro, I just fell in love," Brendo replies.

"What!"

"I just legit fell in love."

"Man, don't do this right now. Are you serious?"

"I'm not even joking, bro."

"Guy, you a waste, man," Jose says.

"What's her name?" Jojo asks.

Brendo pauses. It's clear he has no clue.

Jojo shakes his head.

"Whose mans is this?" Jose says, laughing.

"Chill," Jojo says.

"I'm aight," Brendo reassures them. "But wait till you see her."

The three boys make their way through the party.

Brendo taps Jojo's shoulder. "That's her, the tall blonde. Three o'clock."

"What is three o'clock? Can you just point?" Jojo asks.

Brendo points. Jojo turns and spots a tall blonde girl wearing pine-green Jordans. But then he looks to the girl standing next to her. Suddenly, his heart skips a beat. He can feel his heart flutter in his chest, and the sensation is making his legs feel heavy.

"Wh-who's her friend, though?" Jojo asks.

Jojo can't take his eyes off the caramel-skinned, athletic-looking girl with curly black hair. He likes her style — a Kyle Lowry OVO Raptors jersey and a sick pair of Jordan Bred elevens.

"Oh, those two," Jose says. "That's just Kim Smart and Ashley Vasquez. They're in my homeroom. They're hoopers on the girls' Varsity Squad. Dog, Vasquez is like going D1. She's nice, bro. Fine, too."

"Her? D1? You sure?" Jojo asks, impressed that the girl plays basketball at such a high level. But Jose is already out of earshot as he walks up to the girls.

"Hey, Jose!" Kim shrieks.

"What's goody?" Jose smiles.

"Congrats on making the Squad," Kim says.

"Yeah, respect." Ashley says.

"Are those your friends?" Kim asks.

"The ones you're always talking about?" Ashley says.

"Yeah. That's my Squad."

Jose can see Kim is staring at Brendo.

"Kim, I'll introduce you if you promise to introduce me to Liz in our homeroom."

"Liz?" Kim says.

"Yeah, she here? She so fly."

"Jose, you kill me," Ashley giggles. "But, no, Liz couldn't make it tonight."

"Deal," Kim replies to Jose's offer. Ashley gives Kim a strange look.

Jose waves to Jojo and Brendo to come over.

Jojo turns to Brendo and stops him with his hand on his chest. "Don't be talking about no love stuff." He pokes his finger into Brendo's chest.

"Chill. I got it, bro."

Jose introduces the boys. "These are my guys, Jojo and Brendo."

"What's up?" Brendo says to both, but he locks eyes with Kim.

Kim returns the look. "We were just heading to go to the —"

"We going to hit the courts?" Brendo breaks in.

"How the hell?" Jojo says under his breath. He sees the instant chemistry between Kim and Brendo. Kim turns away and giggles with Ashley. Brendo looks like he is on cloud nine.

Jojo moves closer and nudges his friend. "Chill, guy. Pump your breaks."

"Okay, let's go," Kim says, pulling Brendo by the arm.

Brendo looks back at Jojo and gives him the MJ shrug.

Ashley shakes her head and smiles as her friend leaves with Jojo's friend.

"So —" Jojo starts but he can't find any more words.

"So, congrats on making the Squad," Ashley says.

"Yeah, thanks. You too." *Stupid. Why would you say that?* Jojo thinks to himself. He tries to regain his composure. "So I heard you can shoot. We should play buckets."

Ashley smiles a big toothy grin. "Really?"

"I mean, if you're not scared." Jojo blurts out.

"Well, I don't miss much. So, not scared." Ashley says.

"Oh, okay, listen to Little Miss Too Good here," Jojo says sarcastically. "You're not that good."

Ashley's face suddenly turns serious. She seems offended.

Jojo moves in closer and purposely towers over Ashley. Then he bumps into her playfully. "Uh, weight room." Jojo forces a laugh, trying to lighten the mood.

"Hey!" Ashley shoves Jojo back. "You really want this smoke? Aight, bet," Ashley says, her face dead serious. She charges out of the house towards the outdoor basketball courts.

Jojo stands there for a moment, dumbfounded. What just happened? One moment he was flirting with her and the next moment she was trash talking and ready to play one-on-one? How did he offend her?

Jose runs up and wraps his arms around Jojo. "I see you, big Jo. Shoot your shot, bro."

"Word. I think we might be vibing too," Jojo says, trying to sound confident.

Jojo and Jose make their way to the court. Dozens of kids run ahead of them to the court, and dozens more trail behind.

"A lot of people are going to the courts. What's with all the buzz?" Jojo asks.

Jose's phone keeps buzzing. When he finally looks at it, he holds it up to Jojo. "Yo, you might want to take a look at this snap from Jazz."

Jojo looks at Jose's phone: *Ashley about to put on a show. Some dude say he want all the smoke!*

4 Humble PIE

"Someone has challenged Ashley," Jose says. "Jojo, tell me that's not you."

Jojo shrugs his shoulders.

"Guy, what are you doing? You challenged Ashley Vasquez? Have you lost your mind?" Jose asks.

"It ain't that serious. We just playing."

"I can't believe you're doing this right now. Why?"

As Jojo and Jose enter the park, they see it's packed with kids. Two Black guys from the varsity football team run over.

"Yo, who's playing Ashley?" one asks.

"*Him?*" says the other.

They point at Jojo and start laughing.

There is a commotion, people clamouring to get to the court.

Jojo looks nervously at all the kids gathered around. He sees all the cameras recording. He looks at Ashley, thinking she might call the whole thing off. But instead, she just kneels down to tighten the laces on her shoes.

Jojo can overhear the conversations in the crowd. All of them say that Ashley is about to kill some fool.

"What's happening?" Jojo asks, turning to Jose.

"RIP, bro."

"Dog, chill, we ain't playing for real. Are we?"

"Look around. This for real, homie. You better represent."

Jojo steps onto the court. Many people gather to watch, and everyone has their phone out.

Jojo begins to feel anxious. He wouldn't mind this kind of attention when he's on the court. But he gets the feeling that this crowd knows something he doesn't.

"I just don't get why," Jose says. "Why would you challenge Ashley Vasquez?"

"It was a joke, bro. But c'mon, I have a foot on her, how good can she be?" Jojo asks.

Out of the corner of his eye, Jojo can see Brendo making out with Kim Smart behind the crowd.

"I got this," Jojo whispers to himself.

"I'll shoot for ball," Ashley says.

A little panic begins to set in for Jojo as Ashley removes her jersey. Beneath it, she wears only a black tank and a gold chain with a cross on it. Jojo stares at her as she ties her hair back. Jojo's head is spinning, she looks so good and so scary at the same time.

Ashley hoists the shot up from well behind the three-point line with perfect form and swishes it.

"Check."

"I can't watch this," Jose says to himself. But he can't turn away.

Jojo checks the ball. Right away, Ashley hoists up another three. Her release is flawless. *Swack!* The ball splashes through the net.

"Face," Ashley says nonchalantly.

"Oooh!" The crowd shouts.

Jojo can feel his face getting hot. "Okay, no more space for you," he says, digging into a defensive stance.

"I create my own space," retorts Ashley.

"Oh lawd, she talking," Jose says.

Ashley does a Texas crossover and the move stuns Jojo. He takes a few steps back. Then Ashley looks like she is going to drive it hard to her right. But instead, she quickly crosses the ball over to her left. At this, Jojo feels his balance leave him. He looks at Ashley, hoping that she will show mercy. He sees her eyes light up. She pushes Jojo's hip and crosses him over.

This time, Jojo's knee buckles.

"Aaah," Jojo says, clutching his knee.

"Ooooh!" The crowd goes crazy.

Jojo is falling. He hears the crowd yell, "oooh" again when he hits the ground.

And then . . .

Swack! The sound of the ball ripping through the net.

The crowd erupts again. Everyone is going crazy and rushing the floor. Jojo isn't completely sure what happened, but from the look on Jose's face, it was bad, very bad.

Ashley is standing well behind the three-point line, her hand in a gooseneck follow-through. Phones and their owners are clamouring all around her.

Jojo has never felt this type of humbling on the court — the worst has happened. He is no doubt already on some highlight reel of guys getting "ankle broken."

Jojo starts thinking about how he could play off the negative popularity and get more looks at his profile. He rubs his knee.

Through a tiny seam in the crowd gathered around Ashley, Jojo can clearly see her face. He sees her look through the same seam, directly at him. The two lock eyes just for a moment. And the seam closes.

Jojo pulls out his phone and searches for Ashley's Instagram page.

Jose runs over to help Jojo to his feet. "Bruh, she's got like ten thousand followers. Everyone saw that."

"This girl has taken so many lives," Jojo says, scrolling through Ashley's Instagram. "Look at these videos."

Jojo feels like he's going to faint. All over Ashley's page are videos of her dominating in one-on-one games. They show her taking on all comers — girls, guys, grown men, even. There are some in-game highlights, too, and those are even more spectacular.

Jojo realizes that Ashley Vasquez is the real deal. Ashley is a hooper.

"Bro, how am I going live this down?" Jojo asks Jose.

Jose holds up his phone for Jojo to see. The video was already playing throughout the 'Gram.

"You just another statistic, bro," Jose says.

"Nah. She got me messed up." Then he shouts, "I ain't going out like this!"

5 Coach P Is TRIPPING

In the locker room before practice, several players on the team are watching the video of Ashley breaking Jojo's ankles. Jojo's teammates are having a good time poking fun, especially Ram, Jazz and Harmon.

"Jojo, you need extra tape for those ankles or nah?" Jazz asks.

"That knee, though?" Harmon blurts out.

Harmon and Ram high-five each other and laugh with Jazz.

"How the hell you guys make the Squad anyway? Ya'll are trash," Jojo snaps back.

"At least we didn't get murked by Ashley," Jazz counters.

"You saying you could guard her?" Jose says, coming to Jojo's defense.

Harmon, Jazz and Ram stop laughing.

"That's what I thought," Jose says.

"Just ignore them, Jojo," Brendo says.

Jojo tries to ignore it all. He gets dressed as fast as

he can. "I'll meet you guys out there," he says as he quickly exits the locker room.

Jojo has been dealing with the embarrassment all day at school. It feels like everywhere he goes, someone is playing that video. The only cool part is that he has gained a thousand more followers.

As he walks out onto the court, the girls' team finishes practice. Jojo watches as Ashley towels off on the sideline. Jojo couldn't help but notice Ashley's six pack and her toned arms. She's in perfect shape. He feels his heart flutter in his chest.

Ashley makes her way towards him. Jojo doesn't know what he's going to say to her, after she embarrassed him. He wasn't sure if she'd even want to talk to him.

A big smile spreads across Ashley's face as she walks towards Jojo.

"Hey," Jojo says quietly.

"Hey," Ashley keeps smiling and walks right past him like he's a statue.

Jojo enjoyed the interaction. Is Ashley messing with him? He can't tell. But whatever she is doing makes him want more interactions with her.

"Yo, how about I hit you up later?" Jojo calls after her.

"DM me." she says and leaves the gym.

Jojo stands there, stunned. When he realizes what she said, he can barely contain his excitement. He runs over and jumps on Brendo's back.

"I'm in, man!" Jojo shouts.

"With who? Ashley?"

"Bruh, pure finesse!" Jojo screams.

"Oh, word!" Jose says.

Jojo starts freestyling. "Uh ankle broken, ain't no joking. They hating on him, but I ain't hiding, bounce back, on track, into the DM I'm sliding!"

The three boys start dancing on the court.

Tweet!

In their excitement the boys didn't see Coach Pritchard enter the gym. There he is, standing with his arms crossed and with an angry look on his face.

"So this is what we're doing now? Instead of getting ready for practice, we're *Dancing with the Stars*, is that it, Mr. Antwi?"

Jojo straightens up. "Uh, no Coach."

"Everyone on the baseline."

The boys hustle to the baseline.

Coach Pritchard stares at the team. "This is not recreation ball. If you want to fool around, go play at the YMCA."

Coach turns to stare directly at Jojo. "This isn't *Canadian Idol*, Mr. Antwi."

Jojo looks around. He wasn't the only one fooling around, everyone was. Why is Coach singling him out again?

"I selected each one of you to this team for a purpose," Coach goes on. "We have a common goal and that is to get better every day. And if we're lucky, if we work hard enough, we might have a chance to do something special. But we need to get serious. And that starts with you, Mr. Antwi. I expected you to be a leader."

Jojo makes a face and rolls his eyes.

Coach Pritchard takes a step towards him. "You got something you want to say?"

"We're just having some fun, Coach."

The gym goes silent.

"Fun is getting to practice early and working on your game before practice starts. Okay, Mr. Fun Guy, three-man weave. I want clean passes, no misses."

Tweet!

Jojo, Brendo and Jose go first. Jojo passes to Brendo and sprints up the floor, Brendo passes to Jose, who passes it back to Jojo, who is sprinting up the sideline. Jojo catches the ball and bobbles it. He rushes the layup and misses it.

Tweet!

"Passes need to be on time and on target, Mr. Santos."

"Make a better pass," Jojo whispers to Jose. Somehow Coach Pritchard hears it.

"Jojo, why are you missing layups when there's no defense? Then you blame your teammate? Unacceptable. Everyone on the baseline. You have two sets of lines."

As they run the lines, Jojo can feel his chest start to burn.

"Pick up the pace, Jojo! No more bad passes and no more misses!" Coach yells.

The boys restart the drill and this time, Jose, Brendo and Jojo complete the layup. Then it's the turn of the next group of boys — Ram, Harmon and Jazz. Jazz makes a bad pass to Ram. The ball bounces off Ram's foot and skirts out of bounds.

"Arrgh, what the hell are you guys doing!" Jojo yells.

Tweet!

Jojo expects Coach Pritchard to tear into Jazz. So he is surprised when the coach turns to focus on Jojo.

"Is that the way you encourage your teammate? That's unacceptable, Mr. Antwi. If we can't support each other in this drill, then we'll support each other in another way. Everyone get against the wall."

The boys all run to find a spot on the wall.

Coach checks his wristwatch. "Get into a wall stance, we're in it for a minute. We'll start when everyone is in a stance against the wall. Heels up, butts off the wall. The only thing touching the wall should be your shoulder blades. Get your hands up above your shoulders! Let's go!"

Coach Pritchard walks around, checking everyone's stance.

Jojo can feel his legs shaking. He is struggling to stay in the stance and so are the rest of the boys.

"Thirty seconds more." Coach Pritchard stops in front of Jojo. "What kind of stance is this? Bend your knees, get down low and get your hands up high."

Jojo tries, but his legs keep buckling, and he has to come out of his stance.

"Thanks to Mr. Antwi here, we'll have to start it all over again."

The rest of the boys give Jojo an annoyed look.

Another gruelling minute later, the boys' knees are wobbling. Jojo tries his best to think about something other than the wall stance. He thinks of Ashley.

"Everyone off the wall," orders Coach Pritchard. "Since we aren't in shape and since we aren't serious enough to work on our skills, then we'll work on our fitness. Right, Mr. Antwi?"

Jojo is confused. He wonders if Coach is going to pick on him the whole time. He isn't the only one messing up, yet Coach keeps calling him out.

For the rest of practice, Coach Pritchard makes the boys run lines. After the tenth one, the boys are exhausted. Jojo finishes last. He's wheezing and can't seem to catch his breath.

But Coach isn't done with them yet. "Everyone has fifty push-ups and fifty sit-ups. Mr. Antwi, you have sixty of each. Then hit the showers and we're done for the day."

Coach Pritchard leaves the gym as the boys are doing their push-ups and sit-ups.

Jojo struggles to do the sit-ups and push-ups. He can't figure out why Coach is making him do more than everyone else.

Jose and Brendo come over to encourage him. "Let's go, Jojo. A few more and you're done."

Jojo stops doing push-ups. He sits down on the gym floor, exhausted. "Nah, bro. He talking crazy. Coach P is tripping," he says.

If Jojo wasn't sure before, now he is certain that Coach Pritchard is out to get him.

6 Respect the GAME

Jojo rushes to get ready for the Squad's first game of the season. As he looks at himself in the mirror on his bedroom wall, he thinks about Ashley and the mind games she's been playing with him. He DM'd her "what's up," but she didn't respond. Why did she ask him to send her a message if she wasn't going to respond?

Jojo twists his hair. It's wild and dreading, just how he likes it. He wants to look his best when he shows up at the gym. With the viral video still circulating, Jojo needs today to be a day of redemption. He feels he has to ball out. Then maybe everyone will forget about what Ashley did to him.

They better put some respect on my name, Jojo thinks to himself.

★★★

Jojo walks into the gym dressed to impress. The rest of the team is wearing the team-issued Squad hoodie and

Squad sweatpants. Jojo stands out like a sore thumb in his orange Overtime hoodie, black Gucci shorts, a pair of Yeezys and his white AirPods. He hands Jose his phone and strikes a pose. He throws up some signs with his fingers as Jose snaps a picture of him.

"Good look," Jojo says, snatching back his phone. He walks past the bleachers twice to make sure everyone in the gym has seen him, then heads to the locker room. Brendo and Jose follow behind.

"So, you message Ashley?" Jose asks.

Jojo is about to answer when Coach Pritchard appears in front of him.

The coach looks Jojo up and down. "Where's your Squadron team-issue?" he asks. Then he walks away, shaking his head.

Jojo turns to Jose and Brendo. "Game hasn't even started, bro, and already this guy is cheesing me," he says.

As the boys enter the locker room, Jose asks again about Ashley.

Jojo doesn't want to talk about Ashley and changes the subject. "Did you ask Kim, Brendo?"

"Yeah," says Brendo. "Kim said she'll film the game for me."

"Just make sure she sends me the vid, too," Jojo insists.

"Saw Ashley with Kim," Jose adds.

Knowing Ashley is in the stands makes Jojo nervous.

He walks over to Ram, Jazz and Harmon. "Yo, Jazz, this is a big game for me. So look for me, all right?"

Jazz laughs. "Whatever, bro."

As Jojo turns and walks away, he hears Jazz say, "This guy swears he Lebron or something."

At that point, Coach Pritchard walks into the locker room and claps his hands. "Jojo, Jazz, Jose, Brendo and Ram to start. Actually, check that. Harmon, you start for Jojo."

"What?" Jojo says under his breath. He knows he is way better than Harmon. All summer he, Jose and Brendo practised their intro routines. Now Jojo won't even get to do his because he isn't starting. He was hoping to post it. Coach is ruining everything.

"Our team name, Squadron, means a cohesive unit, we wear 'Squad' across our chest because we are a team together. Jojo, if you're part of this team, wear your team-issue to games. That goes for everyone." Coach says. Then he shouts, "Okay, boys, go out there and play hard for each other. And play together!"

"Squad!" The team cheers. Everyone is pumped except Jojo, who barely cheers. During warm-up, Jojo scans the crowd. He sees Kim and Ashley sitting together.

As the starting lineups are called out for the Squad, Jojo stands up and does a popping and locking dance routine with Jose and Brendo. He is hype for Brendo and Jose. But he can't fully enjoy it because he wishes he was starting.

The Squad are playing a team from Hamilton, but Jojo barely looks at the opposing team. He is too focused on what Ashley and Kim are doing in the stands. He can't wait to show out.

Kim better still be filming once I get in, Jojo thinks.

From the opening tip, Hamilton presses the Squad. Brendo wins the tip to Jose and right away two Hamilton defenders swarm Jose. Jose panics and throws a looping pass over to Jazz. Hamilton intercepts and scores.

The Squad players are rattled by the pressure and turn the ball over several times. In the blink of an eye, they are down 6–0.

"Guys, can you please not lose this game in the first five minutes!" Jojo shouts.

The score balloons to 12–0 and Coach Pritchard yells towards the bench, "Antwi, get in there for Harmon."

"That's what I'm talking about," Jojo says. He jumps up off the bench, but walks over to the scorer's table, trying to look as cool as possible.

"Actually, Jojo, sit back down," Coach calls.

"What?"

"When I call your name, you sprint to the table. Sit down."

Jojo walks back to the bench and plops down. "Oh, this is that bull. For real."

"You say something, Jojo?" Coach asks.

Jojo shakes his head.

With just a few minutes left in the first quarter,

with the Squad down 20–6, Coach Pritchard turns towards the bench and points at Jojo. "Get Harmon."

"Finally," Jojo whispers to himself.

This time, Jojo sprints to the table to sub in.

Jose dribbles the ball up the court. He whips it between his legs, then he flips a no-look pass to Jojo.

"Run the play!" Coach shouts.

"Nah, I got this." Jojo shoots a three-pointer, but it is off way left.

"What are we doing?" Coach yells.

Brendo grabs the rebound and passes it back to Jojo. This time, Hamilton double-teams Jojo.

"Move the ball!" Coach Pritchard shouts.

Instead of passing, Jojo forces the dribble through two defenders. The ball is stolen and Hamilton races down the court and scores.

"Time out!" Coach Pritchard shouts.

The boys come back to the bench where Coach is waiting. He slams his playboard down on the ground and gets into Jojo's face. "You think it's all about you out there?"

"No," Jojo whispers.

"What are we doing then? Run the play!"

The Squad hustles to the court, but to more of the same selfish play. First Jazz forces up a bad shot, then Jose does the same thing, and then Brendo.

By the end of the first half, the Squad is down by twenty points.

As the boys walk into the locker room, Jojo claps his hands in frustration. "You guys need to start getting me the ball. For real!"

As Jojo is talking, Coach Pritchard storms into the locker room and kicks a locker. "Selfish! That's all I see out there, selfish play. No energy, no intensity. And no leadership from anyone, especially from you." Coach Pritchard stares right at Jojo.

Jojo tries to tune out Coach. He thinks about how he hasn't scored yet, and he is desperate to get highlights he can post. And the thought of playing badly makes him feel anxious, because Ashley is watching and Kim is filming the whole thing.

For the second half, Coach starts Jojo instead of Harmon. Early in the third quarter, Jojo finds his rhythm. He grabs a rebound and scores. Then he steals a pass and sprints on a breakaway and scores with a layup. But by the end of the third quarter, the Squad is down by fifteen. In the fourth quarter, Jojo hits a few more shots, but it seems every time Hamilton has the ball, they score.

"Communicate, compete! You can't just let them score," Coach Pritchard keeps shouting.

The game slips away and when the final horn rings, Hamilton has won by twelve points.

Even though his team lost, Jojo can't wait to see the footage. He knows he has a few highlights to post on social media that are guaranteed to get views and likes. Jojo smiles to himself. The game wasn't a complete loss.

Coach Pritchard storms into the locker room. "What on earth are you happy about, Antwi?"

Jojo wipes the smile from his face and pretends to look sombre.

"We just got our tails kicked and you're smiling like the Joker," continues Coach.

Here we go, Jojo thinks. *Time for Coach Pritchard to blame everything on me.*

"You just don't get it, do you, Antwi? This team needs you to lead. I need you to lead. I need you to buy in, respect the game."

Jojo can't take it. Other than Brendo, he had the most points on the team. "I dropped fifteen, Coach," he says quietly.

"Oh, and that's leadership? You could have scored zero points. But if you competed, if you committed to playing the right way — rebound, play defense, be a leader out there . . . " Coach Pritchard pauses. "You know what? Everyone up on your feet. Meet me out on the court."

"You just had to say something, didn't you, Jojo?" Jazz says angrily.

The boys slowly march out to the court.

"On the baseline," Coach barks.

Tweet!

Coach Pritchard makes the team run several lines

with no break in between. After the tenth line, he looks at Jojo.

Jojo expects him to say something negative. Instead, Coach just nods his head. "Practice is at seven a.m. tomorrow morning," he says and walks out.

Jojo rips off his jersey and storms off to the showers.

7 The THREE Ps

Early the next morning, Jojo walks into the locker room. He's physically and emotionally drained. Instead of preparing for practice, he opens his phone and looks at his highlights from the night before. Jojo sees lots of likes and starts scrolling through the comments. A lot of people are commenting about how the Squad lost.

"It's always the biggest haters talking trash in the comments," Jojo says.

"No cap," Brendo says.

"Yo, man, it's already five minutes to seven," Jose says.

Still half asleep, Jojo nods his head.

Brendo taps Jojo on the shoulder. "Ashley was talking about you yesterday."

Jojo makes a skunk face and covers his nose. "Bro, your breath is stank, oh my god."

"Oh yeah?" Brendo cups his hands and smells his own breath.

"Let me smell," Jose says.

Brendo blows air in Jose's direction.

"Brush your teeth, bro," Jojo says.

"I just woke up. My bad," Brendo says. "Anyways, Ashley said you didn't message her."

"That's cap," Jojo says, yawning.

"Well, what account of hers did you message?" Brendo asks.

"What account?" Jojo repeats.

"Yeah, she has a few." Brendo scrolls through his phone. "Her hoops one and then her other one, then her other one. This is her, too. I don't think she checks the others."

Jojo looks at the account. "Damn, that's a hot pic of her. She can dance too." Jojo scrolls through some more reels.

Jojo realizes that he messaged the wrong account. No wonder she didn't respond.

By the time Jojo gets on the court, it's 7:02 a.m.

Coach Pritchard is already on the court, waiting. "Do you know why we lost yesterday?" he asks the team.

"Because we played like trash," Jose says.

"Okay, but do you know why you play like trash?" Coach probes.

Because you didn't start me, Jojo thinks to himself.

"It's because you aren't ready to compete. There are three Ps in basketball that are essential. Does anyone know what they are? Mr. Santos, can you tell what the three Ps are?"

"Uh, passing, posting and positioning," Jose guesses.

Jojo snickers.

Coach glares at Jojo. "No, but decent try. Think about baking cookies."

"Cookies!" Jojo whispers to Brendo. Brendo muffles a laugh.

"When you bake cookies, you have your ingredients — your flour, your sugar, your baking soda, your chocolate chips. Leave out any of the key ingredients and your cookies are, as you say, trash. The three Ps are the ingredients that go into winning. They are preparation, punctuality and perseverance."

Jojo rolls his eyes.

"So when I see guys show up late to practice, Jojo, that's a fail for punctuality. You should be here ten to fifteen minutes early, working on your game. In basketball, and life, much of success has to do with just showing up on time, ready — that's punctuality. You're either early, or you're late. And being ready ties into preparation."

Coach pauses. "Hey, Jojo."

"Yes, Coach."

"Do you shoot three hundred to five hundred shots every day?"

Jojo shakes his head. "No. Not every day." He can't remember ever shooting that many shots in a day.

"Hoopers do that, maybe more. All you see is the finished product of their preparation. Now, I bet none of you shoot that many shots a day. But you all want to jack up bad shots instead of moving the ball for a good shot. That's a lack of preparation. Also, we're not in shape — Hamilton exposed that weakness. Again, that's a lack of preparation in the off season. Which brings me to the last P, which is the most important. Perseverance. Brendo, how does perseverance apply to basketball?"

Brendo's face is blank.

The boys snicker. Jojo doubts that Brendo knows what perseverance even means.

"Uh, it means we just keep playing no matter what happens, or something?"

"Good one," Jojo teases.

"Actually, he's right," Coach Pritchard says. "When we started losing, we lost our intensity and we started blaming each other. Then we fell apart. You have to stay the course. You have to persevere and maintain your mental focus. So, instead of arguing about who is getting the ball, Jojo, we should have been talking about getting back on defense and running our plays."

Jojo rolls his eyes. He knew Coach would find a way to blame him.

"Let's go over our continuity offense," Coach says. "Everyone to your positions. Jose, Jojo, Brendo, Jazz and Ram, you're the first five."

"Finally, some respect," Jojo says under his breath. He usually enjoys playing basketball, but the way Coach is always on him changes things for him — the game has started to feel like a chore.

Throughout practice, the boys work on their plays. Coach Pritchard watches carefully and is quick to jump on anyone who makes a mistake.

Jojo is trying to follow the plays, but none of the plays seem like they end up with him scoring. Frustrated, Jojo catches the ball, drives it to the hoop and scores.

Tweet!

Coach Pritchard marches over. "What was that?"

"It was open, so I took it," Jojo says.

"I know that, but why? We're trying to run the play."

"But, Coach, aren't we trying to score?"

"This is where I need you to be smart. You driving the ball after one pass isn't always going to get it done against the good teams. We need ball movement and man movement."

Jojo shakes his head, fighting back his frustration. Coach Pritchard always has a way to put him down.

Coach reads Jojo's mood. "You better check that attitude, kid. Your body language is negative. Fix it or I will cut you from this team so fast it will make your head spin. Run it again, this time all the way through."

Jojo gives a screw face to Jose and Brendo like he's had enough.

"Chill, bro," Brendo whispers.

At the end of practice, Coach Pritchard makes everyone run lines. Jojo finds that it's easier to run them than before. But he still hates every minute of it. At least thinking about Coach and how much he dislikes him helps take his mind off running.

★★★

At lunch time, Jojo sits in the cafeteria, upset about how things are going with Coach Pritchard. Brendo and Jose join him.

"You good?" Jose asks Jojo.

Jojo doesn't answer. He dips his spoon into some pudding, but puts it back down.

"You think Coach hates me or something?" Jojo asks.

"Nah, he's an equal opportunity hater," Jose says.

"I thought you were going to spaz on Coach in practice. You were heated, bro," Brendo says.

"Man, I can't with that dude." Jojo looks at his phone.

"None of us can," Brendo says.

"This guy is killing my career," Jojo complains. "It's like he don't know that I do this."

"Chill," Jose says.

"Nah, for real, though, I dominated in grade eight. Y'all know I'm finna go D1. And this guy doesn't even start me? Then he wants to look at me in practice like it's my fault we lost or something? Man, screw him, I should just play JV." Jojo says.

"Chill bro. He's like that to all of us," Jose points out.

"C'mon, bruv? Really? You know this guy has had it out for me since day one."

"He ain't lying," Brendo offers.

"I got people trolling my highlights, talking about why I didn't play more. And why Coach is always yelling at me. That's bull." Jojo tosses his phone onto the table.

"Bro, I feel you," Jose says. "My game is freestyle, y'all know this. I need to get into my bag, but it's hard to hoop when he's yelling the whole time. It's throwing me off."

"Yo, forget about Coach," Brendo says. "I got some new bars for our song."

"Word, me too. Let's spit real quick," Jose says.

"I don't know if I'm in the mood to flow, guys," Jojo says.

"Channel that rage, bro. Check this verse I been working on." Jose stands up. "Yo, yo, every time I run up on you, you start crying and don't know what to do. I'm mixing moves like Harden do, step backs slick, flick of the wrist, that's a three, now I'm yelling on you. My moves so sick now you got the flu."

Jojo raises an eyebrow — he's not in the mood but Jose's verse was flames.

Brendo stands up. "I got the rock, now you on the clock. Watch me dance but this ain't TikTok. You yelling please make him stop, but I'm flying straight to the cup making bodies drop, yup!" Brendo raps.

Jojo is starting to feel it, Brendo's verse has him pumped.

Jojo jumps in. "I'm all world in this game and he know it. He trying to tame me, bench me, hoping I blow it. But he can't see me, can't be me, can't teach me how to ball. And if he test me, say less G, I'm slapping Coach P, till he fall, no cap y'all."

Jose and Brendo look at each other.

"Yo, that was straight savage, J," Jose says.

"For real," Brendo says.

"But we can't put that in our song, bro," Jose says.

"I know, but it felt good, though," Jojo says, managing a laugh.

8 Can I LIVE?

Westwood gym is jam-packed with screaming teenagers and parents. It's the Squad's second home game of the season.

In the locker room, Jojo overhears Jose telling Brendo how both his parents and grandparents are at the game. So are Brendo's. Jojo knows that neither of his parents will be in the stands. He stopped wishing for them to come to his games a long time ago.

The locker room is unusually quiet. Even Jazz, Harmon and Ram are silent, with focused looks on their faces. Coach Pritchard marches in with an intense look on his face that is far less angry than usual. "You guys are prepared. Go play together and for each other," Coach says. Then he turns and walks out.

Jose starts a rhythmic drum beat on the lockers. Jojo starts feeling it. They've worked on this pre-game routine all summer.

"We ready, we ready, we reaaaaady for war!" Jojo hoped the rest of the team would join in, but no one does. Jojo stops singing.

"Lame, guys," Jose says.

"Let's go get this!" Jojo yells. The boys charge out of the locker room.

During warm-up, Jojo sees Ashley and Kim in the stands. He tries to focus on the game, but he can't help but notice how nice Ashley looks. Jojo, Jose and Brendo do their dance routine for the starting lineups. The crowd loves it and cheers. Jojo sees Kim and Ashley cheering also.

Pumped up, the Squad charges onto the court to face the Eagles, a team from Vaughan. Jojo wins the tipoff easily. He taps the ball to Brendo, who drives it to the hoop for an easy layup.

The crowd erupts in applause.

The boys search for their checks as they try to press the Eagles.

"Communicate! Who's got ten?" Coach Pritchard yells.

Ten? Jojo's head is on a swivel looking for number ten. By the time he finds the Eagles player, the ball is in his hands. Jojo can hear Coach Pritchard yelling at him, but he blocks it out. He runs full speed at number ten, arms flailing. Number ten panics and throws a wild pass in Jojo's direction. Jojo steals the pass and takes off dribbling to the basket. Brendo is running on his left and he can see Ram on his right. It's a three-on-one with just one defender to beat.

"There they are, see it!" Coach Pritchard yells from the bench.

Jojo fakes the pass to Brendo and steamrolls through the defender, knocking him onto his back. Then he flicks the ball up and kisses it off the glass and into the hoop.

Tweet!

The referee signals to count the basket and calls a blocking foul on the Eagle's defender.

"And one!" Jojo yells, flexing. Jose runs up and jumps on his back.

The Eagles' coach storms in, swearing at the ref and throws his towel onto the court.

Tweet!

The referee calls a technical foul on the coach and threatens to throw him out of the game if he doesn't calm down.

During the commotion, Coach Pritchard calls the boys over. "We have to think! Jojo, that was a dumb play. We're lucky the ref blew the call. Play smarter."

Jojo can't believe it. Somehow Coach has found a way to turn his good play into a negative.

From that point on, the Squad dominates the game. It's clear that the Eagles are no match for them. The Squad players are much faster and stronger than the Eagles, and Jojo is the tallest and biggest player on the court.

In the second quarter, an Eagles player drives the ball to the basket and puts up an under-handed scoop shot. Jojo times the shot and spikes it out of bounds.

"Give me that!" Jojo yells.

"Keep it in play!" yells Coach Pritchard.

Jojo ignores his coach's words. He is done with Coach's hate on his talents. Jojo makes up his mind that any shot that he can get to, he is going to send it into the stands. *Keep it in play,* Jojo scoffs to himself.

By the third quarter, the Squad are routing the Eagles. Jose steals the ball and throws it between the legs of an Eagles player. The crowd gasps and rises to their feet.

Jojo is sprinting down the left side of the court.

"Hit me, Jose!" Jojo calls.

Jose's ball-handling is amazing. He hits the next defender with a bulldog dribble and blows right by him. He spins around the next defender, fakes the pass with his right hand to Jojo and does a scoop layup with his left hand to score.

The crowd goes nuts.

"Okay, Jose!" Jojo yells, getting hype. Jojo feels it is his turn to show out. He charges at the point guard.

"Stay on your man!" Coach Pritchard yells.

Jojo ignores him. As he charges, the point guard tries to throw a pass over Jojo. It is a weak pass and Jojo jumps up and steals it easily. But instead of going in for the uncontested score, Jojo waits until the Eagles player recovers to guard him.

"Why?" Coach Pritchard yells.

"Come get this work," Jojo trash talks. He dribbles

the ball and makes a series of shoulder fakes while dribbling between his legs.

The crowd rises to their feet, sensing a big move is coming. Jojo feels all eyes in the gym focused on him. He knows Ashley is watching and, for just a moment, he gets nervous. The ball squirts loose. In a surprise desperation move, the Eagles' point guard dives after the basketball.

The crowd gasps.

Jojo recovers the ball and does a spin move as the Eagles player flies past him, landing face first on the hardwood. Jojo skips to the hoop, wraps the ball behind his back and lays it in for the score.

"Whew!" Jojo shouts.

The crowd is going crazy in the stands. Jojo cups his hand to his ear as he runs past the crowd.

Tweet!

Coach Pritchard calls a substitution time out. As Jojo runs past the scorer's table, Harmon grabs him by the arm.

"I got you," Harmon says.

"You got me for what?" Jojo says.

"Coach told me to sub you. Who do you have, anyway?" Harmon asks.

"Can I live?!" Jojo storms towards the bench. Giving Coach the side eye, he takes the longest possible route to the end of the bench and plops down. He grabs a towel and places it over his head.

The Squad routs the Eagles and wins the game 50–32.

9 The ABCs of BASKETBALL

Jojo's feeling bitter about how Coach had subbed him out. But Jojo is feeling pretty good about his game. He enters the locker room where the boys are celebrating. A speaker blasts a Drake song.

Coach Pritchard walks into the room. "Quiet!" he shouts.

The boys kill the music, but Jose is still dancing.

"Aye, aye," Jose says as he dances like Soulja Boy.

Jazz nudges him to stop. Jose falls over when he sees Coach Pritchard. He quickly jumps back to his feet. "My bad, Coach."

Jojo tries not laugh. But he takes one look at Brendo's face and bursts into laughter, as the rest of the team joins in.

Coach shakes his head and smiles for a second, then his face turns serious. "You know what? Good win and you should feel good. But this was one of those times where we actually got worse in a win."

Jojo can't believe it. Coach Pritchard has to be the

most negative person on the entire planet. *Only he can turn a win into a loss*, Jojo thinks to himself.

"We stopped running our plays. We started playing to the crowd, showing off, playing hero ball and just not playing to our potential. We played down to the level of our opponent. I know you are all just sophomores, but that's unacceptable. I'm disappointed. I'm especially disappointed with your lack of leadership, Jojo."

"Whatever," Jojo scoffs. He didn't mean to say it out loud, but he meant it.

Coach Pritchard stands right in front of Jojo. "Do you talk to your parents like that?"

Jojo shrugs his shoulders.

"Well, we don't talk like that on this team. On this team, we have respect. Respect for our teammates, respect for our coach. We have respect for this game and this program." Coach looks around the room. "Who feels *whatever* about that?"

No one puts up their hand.

"You should have all put up your hands. That is how you played and that's how you act." Coach walks over to the door and holds it open. "Everyone back out on the court. We got ten timed suicides, and you better make your times or I'm doubling it. Let's go!" he shouts.

Slowly, the boys exit the locker room. Jojo is the last one left. Coach Pritchard stands there holding the door open.

"Coming?" Coach asks.

Jojo thinks about telling Coach where he can go and how he can get there. He considers quitting right there and then. But instead, he runs past Coach Pritchard, bumping him slightly on his way past the door.

"My bad," Jojo says.

"Keep that same energy on the court."

Jojo scowls as he runs lines. They just won, and here they are being punished. Is nothing good enough for Coach Pritchard?

★★★

Jojo slaps the padding on the baseline wall so hard that part of the Velcro comes loose. The boys have just finished running their eighth set of lines in practice, and now Jojo's legs are burning.

"This is all we do," Jojo whispers.

"Last one. Ready stance. Go!" Coach Pritchard yells.

Jojo trails behind the rest of the boys. As he coasts to the baseline, he breathes a sigh of relief that at last the running is done.

"Jojo!" Coach yells.

"Yes, Coach P?"

"Wait, what did you just call me?"

"Coach P?" Jojo gulps hard.

"Okay, I like that. Jojo, tell me, why are you okay with finishing last?"

Jojo shrugs his shoulders. "We're not competing," Jojo says.

"All of you just coasted. Jojo, you barely ran at all. And you're right, it's because you're not competing. Have you ever heard of the ABCs of basketball?"

The team is silent.

"Run to the baseline and back," Coach orders. "The last one back has twenty push-ups."

Tweet!

The boys take off running. Jojo stumbles and falls. He picks himself up and hustles, but still finishes last. He drops to the ground and starts doing his push-ups.

"Can anyone guess what the A in the ABC stands for?" Coach Pritchard asks.

"Aggressive!" Jose yells out.

"Wrong. Everyone do thirty jumping jacks. Last person done has twenty push-ups."

Jojo is on his fifteenth push-up. By the time he gets to his feet and starts the jumping jacks, the rest of the team has finished.

"The A stands for Always," Coach says.

Jojo finishes his jumping jacks and starts on his push-ups.

"Can anyone guess what the B stands for?" Coach asks.

Ram puts his hand up. Coach Pritchard points at him.

"Like, be aggressive and be tough," Ram says.

The whole team groans.

"Worst answer of all time," Jojo jokes, pausing from his push-ups.

For a moment, Jojo can feel Jazz staring at him. Jojo stares Jazz down until Jazz refuses to make eye contact.

"Ram is actually correct. It stands for Be. Everyone except for Ram has a down and back. Last one back has thirty sit-ups and twenty push-ups," Coach says.

"Yeah! Shows how much you know," Jazz shouts in Jojo's ear as he runs past.

This is all Coach's fault for picking on me, Jojo thinks. *He's making me look weak.* Jojo finishes his last push-up as the boys take off running. He scrambles to his feet and runs as hard as he can. He doesn't want to finish last again.

Jazz slips on the baseline and Jojo sees his chance to catch up. He sprints his hardest. Jazz bounces back to his feet quickly. Seeing Jojo catching up, he too sprints as hard as he can.

The rest of the team cheers the boys on.

"Go, Jazz!" Harmon yells.

"You got him, Jo," Brendo shouts.

Jojo and Jazz are in a dead heat sprint back to where the rest of the team is gathered. Jazz has a half a step lead on Jojo as they near the line. In desperation, Jojo dives headfirst across the line.

Jojo looks up to see Coach Pritchard standing over him. "Well done, boys," Coach says. "But I think that's twenty, Jojo."

"What? I won!" Jojo says.

"Is that how you feel, Jazz?" Coach asks.

"Heck, no. I beat him, Coach."

Harmon and Ram start clapping their hands for their champion.

"Of course you take his side," Jojo whispers. He should have known Coach would rig this against him. But instead, Coach hands a basketball to Jojo.

"Well, boys, I guess we'll have to have a shootout to decide this." He looks into Jojo's eyes. Jojo thinks he might see a smile, but then it's gone.

"First person to miss two in a row loses," Coach says.

Right away, Jose is in Jojo's face. "You got this," he says. He punches Jojo several times in the chest. Jojo has never seen Jose this pumped before. He feels energized. He really wants to beat Jazz.

Jazz is jumping up and down with Harmon and Ram, getting really hype.

Jojo steps up to the three-point line and lets the shot fly. *Swish!* The ball splashes through the net.

"Water," Jose shouts.

Jojo holds his follow-through. A feeling of confidence and energy sweeps over him.

Jazz steps up and shoots with excellent form. Jojo knows Jazz is arguably the best shooter on the team. Still, Jojo believes he can beat Jazz, and he has to. Ashley was one thing, but Jazz is one person he can't stomach losing to.

Swish! Jazz's shot ripples the net.

"Waterfalls," Ram shouts.

Jojo steps up and makes his next shot, and then he makes two more.

"Glaciers," Brendo says.

"He said glaciers," Jose says laughing hysterically.

Jojo is starting to surprise himself at how well he is shooting. He can't remember ever making this many in a row under pressure. But Jazz keeps pace with him, matching him shot for shot.

Jazz steps up and shoots. His ball rattles around the rim and then pops out.

"No!" Jazz yells.

"Yes!" Jose yells.

"Wet this!" Brendo yells.

Jojo doesn't break his focus. He takes his next shot.

The ball hits the front rim. It bounces several feet straight up into the air before coming down straight through hoop.

Brendo and Jose jump up and down. "That's what I'm talking about!" Jose shouts.

Jazz takes his shot and misses it.

"That's twenty, Jazz," Coach Pritchard says.

"Yeah!" Jojo shouts at Jazz.

"Learn a lesson. The C in ABC stands for Competing. The ABC of basketball is Always Be Competing. Remember that."

Coach walks over to Jojo.

"You know, the only one stopping you is you." Coach says it quietly so only Jojo hears.

Coach turns to the rest of the team. "All right, get showered up."

Jojo stands there and thinks, *the only person stopping me is you, Coach P.*

10 The Perfect GIFT

"Hell, naw!" Jojo says, as he holds the flower shop door open as him, Brendo and Jose leave. "I am not getting Ashley flowers for Christmas. I might as well go full creep and buy her a ring too."

Brendo has several wrapped roses under his arm, and Jose has a single white rose and a neatly wrapped box of chocolates under his.

"This is stupid anyway," Jojo says.

"Bro, it's first class to give your girl gifts at the Christmas party," Brendo says.

"Act like you know, Jojo," Jose says.

"Y'all talking crazy. She's not even my girl," Jojo says.

"Okay, don't get her anything. See what happens," Jose says.

As the boys walk along the sidewalk, Jojo eyes Jose.

"What I'm tripping on is, since when is Jose the dating expert here?" Jojo asks.

Brendo and Jojo laugh.

"Keep hating, Jojo. But I'm the one who's had three girlfriends. That's three to zero, just saying."

"No cap. Jose is talking to Liz," Brendo says to Jojo.

"I start rappin' and that's how it happens," Jose says confidently.

"Liz from the Squad? Okay, Jose, respect," Jojo says. "You really think I need to get Ashley something?"

"Put it this way," Jose says. "If you don't, someone else will, promise you that."

Jojo thinks about it some more. He has no clue what to get her. "Uh, I'll catch up with you guys at the party tonight." He turns and sprints home. There is at least one person he can ask about what a girl would like.

When Jojo gets home, he runs through the dining room and bursts through into the kitchen. "Mom!" he shouts.

The house is silent.

"The one time I need you. The one time!" Jojo shouts. He punches the fridge in frustration. He thinks about calling his dad but decides against it. His dad works until late every night and rarely answers his phone.

Jojo angrily rips a note off the fridge, spilling magnets all over the pearly kitchen tiles. *Always a note. She can't text?* he thinks to himself.

Jojo reads over the note written in Twi, his mother's native tongue. It says something about jollof leftovers in the fridge. As he reads his mother's note, it occurs to him that he can write something for Ashley, like a poem or song. If it's dope, maybe she'll be impressed.

Jojo sits on one of the barstools at the kitchen island, pulls out his phone and starts typing a note. "You my superstar" – *nah, corny*," Jojo thinks.

Maybe this isn't such a good idea, Jojo starts to wonder. But then, Jojo remembers Coach P's principles. For Jojo, there is something about the ABCs of basketball that has stuck with him. He can't shake it. He can feel the same competitiveness that allowed him to make shots, it's driving him to write something that will win over Ashley. Jojo's imagination starts to race. He pictures Ashley with him on the court, she's melting into his arms as he recites the song.

Jojo takes a deep breath, he closes his eyes and tries to concentrate. *Okay.* Jojo picks up his phone and starts humming an afrobeats tune. As he hums, he writes, "Hey, Ash, I'm no good at gifts, it's true, but I'd like to sing this song to you."

Jojo continues to type feverishly. When he finishes, he reads over the song and smiles. It's perfect.

Later that evening, Jojo, Brendo and Jose arrive at Ram's house. Jojo wears his Kyrie Easter kicks, black Gucci sweatpants and a crisp and clean white T-shirt. He has two diamond studs in his ear. And around his neck is his favourite piece of jewellery — a wooden necklace with shiny beads and a massive wooden

Adrinka symbol hanging from it. He got it from Ghana the Christmas before.

"Damn, Jo, the drip hit different tonight," Jose says. "Your parents just buy you whatever, huh?"

"They better," Jojo mutters. Since his parents separated earlier that year, they are both showering him with everything he could ask for. Everything except their time.

"Bro, you really go all out, huh," Jose nods.

"The swag stays on a trillion," Jojo says.

"One hunnid trillion with this one," Brendo says.

"Huh?" Jojo says.

Ram answers the door. He pretends like he is going to shut the door in their faces. "Ha, I'm just playing. Get in here. This party is lit!" Ram grabs Jojo, hugs him and then gives him the thumbs up.

Jojo nods. He thinks how it is super weird how enthusiastic Ram is acting.

The boys make their way through the party. Brendo heads straight towards the couches in the foyer where Kim and the other Squad girls are hanging out. Jose follows.

Jojo lags behind, looking for Ashley. She hasn't responded since he sent her the song. He checks his phone. It shows no message sent to Ashley. Confused, Jojo retrieves the song from his phone's notepad and hits "send" again. He was certain it said it was delivered the first time he sent it. He scrolls through his phone.

Oh no! Jojo *had* sent the song. But he accidentally sent the message to the Squad group chat, which was set up by the school to communicate practice times and game schedules to the Squad teams. That meant his song went out to every single Squad player and coach, every manager and all of the teacher sponsors, for all the sports at the school.

Brendo presents Kim with the roses, and Kim jumps up and kisses Brendo. Jojo can see Jose presenting the white rose and box of chocolates to Liz, a tall, light-skinned Jamaican girl. Liz hugs him and takes hold of his hand.

Jojo begins to panic. He knows there's a good chance Ashley has seen his message already. Jojo can see the Squad girls looking at him, smiling and laughing. Brendo gives him the thumbs-up. Jojo's head is spinning. *Has everyone seen his text?*

Jojo realizes he may have just torpedoed his chances with Ashley and embarrassed himself. But a plan comes to mind. There's only one way to turn it all around.

The lights go dim all over the party. Harmon and Ram move the couches along the walls and clear out space in the foyer. The DJ starts playing hit after hit, and everyone starts dancing.

Jojo runs up to Jazz. Jazz whips around and immediately wraps his arms around him.

"Get off me, Jazz," Jojo says. "What's the matter with you?"

"Whoa. Relax, bro," Jazz says. "You're my hero. That song, bro. You shooting your shot from the logo."

"Jazz I need a huge favour, are you down?" Jojo asks.

11 BAD READ

Jojo's worst fears are confirmed. Everyone has read his song for Ashley.

"Man, you got some balls," Jazz says. "I know you trying to be a rapper. But damn. Ashley? Respect, bro. I got you on this."

Jojo begins to feel faint. This is why everyone was looking at him. Jojo scans the party. Still no sign of Ashley. If he can get a hold of her before she gets to the party then maybe he can get out this.

Jojo heads for the door. As he passes, he hears a few kids yelling some of his lyrics.

Jojo starts sprinting. Just as he gets outside, he meets Ashley walking up the steps.

"Hey, Jojo," Ashley says.

"Hey," Jojo says. He's thrown slightly by how she looks. She is wearing tight capri pants, a form-fitting white top, pink lip gloss and heels. He's never seen her in anything but athletic gear. Jojo tries to focus, but he can smell her perfume, and the sweet vanilla smell is making his legs feel weak. *She looks just as sweet as she smells*, Jojo thinks to himself.

"Is Kim in there?" Ashley asks. "She has my bag with my phone and all my stuff."

"Oh, why does she have your bag?" Jojo asks.

"I stayed after practice to get in my five hundred."

Jojo can see Ashley's curly hair is wet. His mind is racing. She has come straight from the gym, which means she hasn't seen any of the messages.

"You do that a lot?" Jojo asks, stalling.

"Shoot? Yeah, of course. Every day." Ashley says.

"Look, Ashley," Jojo says. "You can't go in there."

"Why? What now? Is that Jason guy in there?"

"Jason?"

"Yeah, he's this fanboy who likes me or whatever. Apparently he's got like a thousand roses to give me. Or something lame like that."

"You like him?" Jojo asks. *Jose was right.*

Ashley looks Jojo in the eyes. "He's a bit lame. You think maybe I should be nice to him?"

"No, don't!"

Ashley looks at Jojo and smiles.

"I mean. Flowers are lame," Jojo says. "I think Kim's in the foyer. You should check your phone, though, and I'll, uh, see you in a bit."

"Uh, okay, cool," she says. "You okay?"

Jojo does his best to act normal. "Yeah, I'm good. You?"

Ashley makes a confused face and shrugs her shoulders.

As Ashley makes her way into the party, Jojo is already texting Jazz: don't start till I walk in.

Jazz responds with an emoji: 💯

Jojo paces back and forth, preparing his mind, rehearsing the song. He is so nervous his hands are shaking and he can feel his armpits dripping with sweat. This is bound to be filmed. He checks his phone and sees that Ashley has just seen the message. Beads of sweat form on his forehead. Jojo takes a deep breath and makes his way back into the party.

Jojo sees Ashley on her phone. As she reads his song, a perplexed look spreads across her face.

"Did you know about this?" Ashley asks Kim.

Kim shrugs her shoulders.

As Jojo nears the foyer, Jazz cuts the music and drops a catchy instrumental.

Ashley looks up from her phone to see Jojo shuffling towards her. A crowd follows Jojo and forms a semi-circle around him and Ashley.

No turning back now. Jojo catches the beat and starts bopping his head to the rhythm. Ram runs up and hands him a microphone.

"Okay, you the stunna, you see. Hoop game crazy. Can't nobody see... Boss lady genes, the girl of my dreams, okay." Jojo holds his heart as he dances.

The crowd erupts with some cheers. Jojo feels his

confidence rise. He starts waving his arms to get the crowd to start bouncing.

"Aye, girl, okay! I wrote you this rhyme so you can see. I'm feeling your vibe, come roll with me, okay! Just bounce to this, get crunk to this, twerk, twerk, watch me freak."

The Squad boys chant with Jojo.

Jose and Brendo come to Jojo's side and dance along. Jojo feels a confidence he's never experienced before. Jojo shakes his butt in front of Ashley.

Embarrassed, Ashley pushes Jojo away. He doesn't miss a beat, and starts in with an afro-hiplife flow. The crowd starts to cheer.

"Bae, bae, fragile is my heart, for you I give it all up, I want to make you mine oh, slow wind oh, like your game, you so fine oh. You da real stunna make my heart go flutta, dun kno dey wunna, but can't stop da stunna. They wunna but dey can't stop da stunna. They wunna —"

Suddenly, Ashley pushes past Jojo and rushes out of the party. Right away, the cheers die, and the music stops with a screech. The room is silent.

Jojo looks around, puzzled. He sees the reactions of the Squad girls. Their attitude has changed.

"Jerks!" Kim shouts. She walks up and pushes the flowers into Brendo's chest. Then she chases after her friend.

"No, wait!" Brendo says and chases after her.

Liz drops her rose and chocolates. Jose runs up to her to explain, but she kisses her teeth and puts her hand in Jose's face — like *talk to the hand* — and marches out.

Just then, Jojo looks up to see dozens of roses and water falling from the balcony. Some of the roses were artificially coloured and their dye found its way onto the white living room carpet. He looks up and sees a tear-stained face staring back at him. Guess he didn't appreciate the song, either.

"Hey!" Ram shouts. "What the hell?! My parents are going to freak!"

Ram and Harmon sprint up the stairs to find the culprit.

What a disaster, Jojo thinks. He's not sure what happened, but he is sad that he ruined things for Jose and Brendo, too.

Some students try to give Jojo daps and console him for his efforts. But he keeps walking towards the door. He can't stop thinking about Ashley's reaction and the look on her face. She rushed out like she was embarrassed. Jojo remembers their earlier conversation about Jason. Jojo realizes that must have been his tear-stained face and he just showered everyone with roses and soiled Ram's home.

Maybe now Ashley is thinking about how lame I am. What was I thinking?

12 No Excuses, NO EXPLANATIONS

As Jojo runs up the court, he hears Coach P yelling at him to sprint back on defense. But Jojo tunes that out. His attention is focused on Ashley, sitting a few rows up in the stands. She's wearing a bulky sweatshirt and sweatpants, but to Jojo she looks bad to the bone.

Jojo thinks about how he messed up. He put Ashley on blast in front of everyone.

Ashley hasn't texted or said a word to him since then. But there she is in the stands, watching his game. Jojo wants to do something to impress her. He breaks towards the ball, trying to surprise the Brampton Bulldogs' player.

"No!" Coach Pritchard yells.

Keyshawn, a Jamaican boy with dreadlocks, golden skin and a sturdy build, is the Bulldogs' point guard. He calmly dribbles around Jojo. "Foolish!" he shouts to Jojo as he takes off towards the hoop. Brendo tries to prevent the layup, but Keyshawn lobs it just out of his reach.

"On his head!" Keyshawn shouts.

Then Jojo sees Prince Bol, a lanky six-foot-seven Congolese baller with serious hops, ranging towards the hoop.

"Oh, no," Jojo whispers.

Prince elevates and catches the lob. He dunks it on Brendo with so much force that Brendo crumples to the ground. The entire gym explodes in cheers and applause. Some students spill onto the court.

Prince stands over Brendo, tapping his head — basketball sign language to say *I dunked on your head*. Prince is flexing and he's screaming at the top of his lungs like he's powering up like Goku.

Prince tries to stop Brendo from getting back to his feet, but Brendo jumps up and pushes Prince. Prince shoves him back.

Jojo grabs Brendo and pushes him away.

"On your head, white boy!" Prince shouts.

Jojo turns around and shoves Prince with everything he has. Prince stumbles back and falls to the ground.

Tweet! Tweet!

"What!" Jojo shouts at Prince.

With cat-like speed, Prince jumps back to his feet and smiles eerily. His face is just inches from Jojo's.

Jojo sees a crazy look in Prince's eyes. Jojo's heart is racing, and he's scared that Prince Bol might haul off and punch him. But he holds his ground and prepares to defend himself. Where the hell are his teammates? Or the ref? Anyone?

"Y'all trash," Prince says. Suddenly, he steps back and winds up. Jojo braces himself. Suddenly, he feels his body levitate with such force it makes his head spin. When his feet touch back down he turns to see Coach Pritchard, who continues pulling him away towards the bench.

"Easy there, big fella," Coach says. "You don't want it with that kid. He's not the one."

Relief sweeps over Jojo. The referees restrain Prince and escort him back to his bench.

Brendo is still upset. Jojo has never seen Brendo that angry before. Jojo knows that the anger is partially because he lost Kim. She hasn't even come to the game. And Brendo hasn't spoken to Jojo since the party.

While the crowd is still buzzing over the dunk and the scuffle, Jojo looks up at the scoreboard. The Squad is getting beaten by fifteen points, and there are only a few minutes left to play. As he scans the stands, he sees Ashley has left.

In the locker room after the loss, Coach Pritchard stands there, just staring at the team. Except for a few coughs and sniffles, no one makes a sound. Finally, Coach claps his hands, as if coming out of a deep trance. "Listen up."

Coach walks towards Jojo. "This loss today is on you."

Jojo knew he had a really poor game, but so did everyone. Coach always finds a way to make him feel worse.

"And your selfishness got your teammate dunked on," Coach says.

Tears well up in Jojo's eyes as he stares across at Brendo. Brendo refuses to make eye contact.

"You were completely distracted out there, Jojo. And it cost us. What's going on with you?"

Jojo didn't know if he could trust his coach. "I've just been dealing with a lot, Coach P."

Coach takes a step back and looks around the room. "Anyone else in here dealing with a lot? You all certainly played like your heads were somewhere else."

One by one the boys put up their hands. As Ram puts up his hand, Jojo remembers hearing how his parents have grounded him. That red dye found its way onto some very expensive white carpet.

As the whole team puts their hands up, Coach Pritchard crosses his arms. "Let me ask you a question. If your parent's car breaks down and you're late for practice, whose fault is that?"

The boys shout out answers.

"It's no one's fault. The car broke down."

"The car's fault."

"Parent's fault for not maintaining the car."

Coach nods his head. "Wrong, wrong, wrong. Let's try another one. Let's say we are in the playoffs, and the referee is against us because his nephew plays on the other team. He fouls out all our best players and we lose the game. Whose fault is it that we lost?"

"That stupid ref's fault."

"Yeah, the ref's fault, no cap."

"Troll-ass ref."

"Wrong again," says Coach. "How about this — we're in the championship game and Jojo here gets fouled hard and is injured. And then Ram twists his ankle."

"Yo, don't do me like that, Coach," Ram says.

"Okay, then," says Coach. "Let's say Brendo goes knee-to-knee with a guy and he gets hurt. We end up losing the championship by a few points, whose fault is it that we lost?"

"Bad luck."

"That's on God."

"No one's fault."

"Can't control injuries."

"No, you can't control injuries. Or cars breaking down or refs who are against you. But that's always the case. Just like you can't control what's happening in the stands, or sometimes the crazy stuff happening in your life. But that's only an excuse. That's only an explanation. Winners don't have excuses. Winners don't have explanations. Winners just win, no matter what. Losers have excuses. Losers have explanations and reasons why they lost. The question is, are you okay with losing for any reason?" Coach Pritchard asks.

The boys look around at each other.

"Ram? Jose? Are you guys okay with being losers?"

"No, Coach."

"No excuses and no explanations from now on. That goes for everything on and off the court. And you'll commit to that if you want to be winners here and in life, it's called being accountable and taking responsibility. But if you want to feel like this, keep doing what you're doing. Keep getting distracted, keep making excuses. You guys seem to be pretty good at that part." Coach heads towards the door, but stops short.

Jojo couldn't feel worse. He cost them the game and he really screwed over Brendo and Jose, his two best friends. He wishes Coach P would just leave so he could get out of there.

"If there's one positive thing we can take away from this game, it's that we now know when it hits the fan and your back is against the wall, that kid right there — he'll have your back." Coach says. "That's your captain."

Jojo looks up in time to see Coach point at him and then exit. The rest of the Squad players turn to look at him too.

"Yo, Jojo, you put that dude on his back, bro. Jo, you a beast, yo," Jazz says.

Brendo walks over and puts his hand on Jojo's shoulder. "Thanks for having my back."

"Gotchu," says Jojo. "And my bad for —"

"Say less," Brendo says.

The two boys exchange their most complicated handshake, cleanly and with a little extra gusto at the end.

Jose runs up and gives Jojo and Brendo a hug. "All right then, fellas!"

Jojo gives daps to his teammates and rushes out of the locker room.

It's the first time in a long time Jojo is leaving the locker room in good spirits. Coach P singled him out again, but he also named him captain and that helped with his friends. And he also saved Jojo from a certain ass-whooping at the hands of Prince Bol. It doesn't cancel out all the things Jojo is holding against Coach Pritchard, but it makes him wonder if he knows Coach as well as he thinks.

13 JUST QUIT

Jojo, Jose and Brendo are on the court fifteen minutes before practice is supposed to start. To their surprise, so is the rest of the Squad.

Coach Pritchard puts the boys through various individual drills. He demands maximum effort from them. Jojo is feeling exhausted, but he tries to work his hardest. He concentrates on doing the drills correctly so he won't have to interact with Coach P.

But Coach intercepts a pass from Jose to Jojo in the post. "Weak pass, Jose. Even weaker seal, Jojo. Hold your position," Coach tells them.

Then Coach runs over to Brendo. "That's the third layup I've seen you miss. There's no defense on you and you're blowing layups? Blown layups lead to breakouts and buckets for the other team!" Coach P shouts.

Brendo slouches over. His shoulders droop and he puts his head down. Jojo realizes Brendo is a shell of his former self since Kim dumped him.

Coach makes a disgusted face. "What is with your body language, young man? Straighten up! Put your shoulders back! Walk with some confidence, dammit."

Jojo nudges Jose. "Yo I murdered you in 2K last night."

"What? No, dude. Don't talk to me." Jose says.

Coach is still shouting as he walks down the court. "This is the last practice before the winter break and you guys don't even look like you want to be here. Pretenders!"

Jojo knows Coach is right. No one wants to be at practice, including him. But Jojo knows to go hard when Coach is watching.

At the other end of the gym, Coach Pritchard shouts at Jazz, Harmon and Ram to work harder. Jazz rolls his eyes so hard even Coach sees it.

"Uh-oh," Jose says.

"All right, then," Coach says.

Coach storms out of the gym doors. Moments later, he storms back in with tape and black paper. Jojo and the boys watch as Coach Pritchard covers all the gym windows with black paper until they can no longer see out and no one can see in.

Then Coach goes into the janitor's closet and comes out holding two large garbage cans and a mop.

"What the —" Jojo says.

Coach grabs the ball bag and starts stuffing the basketballs away. "On the baseline. Start your suicides.

After each one, do thirty push-ups and thirty sit-ups."

"How many suicides are we doing?" Jojo asks.

"As many as it takes. You see, those garbage cans are for y'all. If anyone needs to throw up, use those garbage cans over there. And mop up any spills."

Tweet!

After the boys finish the third suicide and third set of thirty push-ups and sit-ups, Harmon sprints to the garbage can and throws up.

"Use the mop," Coach Pritchard shouts.

Jojo can feel Coach watching him. Even though he is tired, he blocks it out and keeps running as hard as he can. He doesn't know if he's trying to impress Coach P or if he's trying to prove something. All he knows is that he isn't going to let Coach win.

By the time they reached five suicides and 150 sit-ups and push-ups, the boys are groaning and struggling to go on.

"I can't feel my arms," Jose says.

"You're starting to slow down," Coach says. "So now you have timed suicides. Everyone has to be under thirty seconds or I'm increasing it to fifty sit-ups and fifty push-ups."

Tweet!

The boys run as hard as they can as Coach Pritchard holds his stopwatch.

Jojo is among the first to finish. The boys hunch over, trying to catch their breath. Jojo feels like he's going to pass out, but he fights the feeling.

"Twenty-nine seconds! Get ready, we're going again," Coach shouts.

Jojo sees that Harmon has barely made it. Same with the other boys.

"Harmon's not making this," Jose says.

Ram runs over to the garbage can and throws up.

"Mop!" Coach Pritchard shouts.

Jojo walks over to Harmon. Harmon is gasping for air and shaking his head. "I can't. I'm done, Jo," he gasps.

"C'mon, man" Jojo says. "You got this. We ain't doing those push-ups man."

Tweet!

The boys are off and running.

"C'mon, Harmon!" Jojo shouts.

The boys arc supporting Harmon and cheering each other on with genuine enthusiasm, mixed with desperation. As they finish, Harmon is well behind.

"Twenty-seven, twenty-eight, twenty-nine," Coach counts down.

Harmon is running as hard as he can.

"Run, Harmon!" Jojo yells.

Harmon dives across the line and lies sprawled out on the floor.

"Didn't make it," Coach Pritchard says flatly.

The boys all groan in unison. Jojo walks over and helps Harmon to his feet.

Instead of doing their push-ups, the boys stand there, dejected.

"Oh, so you guys don't want to do the push-ups and sit-ups, is that it?" Coach asks.

The boys remain silent.

"In for a penny, in for a pound. If you guys don't want to do what I'm asking you to do, or if this is too hard, or if you're not having fun, then you can quit. Go home. We're just a bunch of pretenders here anyway. You got five minutes to decide what you're going to do. In or out." Coach swings the ball bag over his shoulder and heads to the equipment room.

"I'm out," Harmon says.

"Me too," Ram says.

"I can't deal with this right now," Brendo says.

One by one the boys declare they are ready to quit.

"Yeah, screw this guy," Jazz says.

Jojo grabs Brendo by his shoulder. "You need to pull it together. If Kim don't want you, it's her loss, bro." Jojo tries to motivate Brendo.

Then Jojo turns to address the team. "I'm not quitting!" he shouts.

Jose moves to Jojo's side. "Me either."

Jojo looks at Jose and smiles. One thing he loves the most about Jose is that Jose is a ride or die friend.

"Guys, this is what he wants," Jojo says. "Coach P wants us to break and punk out. He thinks we're soft."

"Jojo, you get it the worst," Jazz says. "I thought you'd be the first to bounce."

Jojo has to think quickly. Jazz is right, if anyone is going to quit, it should be him. "If we quit now, everything he's said about us being pretenders will be true. Everyone thinks we're a joke, including that guy. I can't give him the satisfaction," Jojo explains.

"Word," Jose says.

Jojo drops to the ground and starts doing the push-ups. Jose joins him.

"I know how we can make him eat his words," Jojo says.

Brendo and then, slowly, the other boys follow Jojo's lead and start doing the push-ups.

14 Real HOOPERS

Jojo adjusts his position on the couch. He's playing video games against the other Squad teammates online. Suddenly, he drops the controller and falls off the couch onto his bedroom floor. His legs convulse with muscle spasms and every time he moves, another muscle flexes. "Ouch! Ouch! Ouch!" Jojo shouts, writhing in pain. Finally, he finds a position where he can stretch out.

While stretching, Jojo sees that he's more flexible than he used to be. He stands up gingerly, and catches his reflection in the floating vanity mirror in his bedroom. Something is different about how he looks. Jojo limps to the washroom.

Immediately, Jojo rips off his shirt and examines his body in the mirror.

"Okay, okay," Jojo says to himself. He's seeing muscles on his chest he's never seen before.

"I'm out here getting cut up." Jojo whispers. Jojo flexes his arms. They look more defined and muscular also. Must be all those push-ups.

Overflowing with confidence, Jojo limps back to his room and grabs his phone. He dials Ashley's number and takes a deep breath as the line trills. He tries out some lines. "*Yo, what's up?* No. *Hey, what up, girl?* Nah. *What's cracking? What it do?* Nah." Jojo shakes his head. What is he supposed to say?

"Hello," Ashley answers.

Jojo hesitates. Then, "Uh, hey, are you mad at me?" he blurts out.

Ashley is quiet. The silence is agonizing for Jojo. Finally she answers, "Why did you do that?"

"My bad. I just, I just wanted to do something nice for you."

"But why did you send it to the group chat?"

"I messed up."

"Yeah, you did. My coach saw that."

Jojo doesn't know what to say. He wasn't thinking about how Ashley would feel about everyone getting the message.

"Rapping was decent," Ashley says. "Dance moves could use some work."

"Oh, so you did like it?"

"You had some bars."

"Then why all the drama with your team? Brendo is heartbroken."

"Mess with one of us, deal with all of us. My girls have my back. Kim especially. That's just how we roll. They'll probably be back together by the end of the week."

"And Liz?" Jojo asks, trying to cover all the bases.

"Pretty sure Liz and Jose have been low-key hooking up."

Jojo laughs. *Wow, Jose,* he thinks. "What about us?" Jojo asks.

"Us?" Ashley asks.

"I mean, I feel like we vibing."

"I don't hook up."

"What's that mean?"

Ashley laughs. "I mean, with school and ball I don't really have time. Especially with someone who isn't hooping."

"Whoa, harsh," Jojo says. "I wasn't even playing for real when you crossed me up."

"Yes, you were playing for real, nice try. Look, I'm not trying to throw shade. You wouldn't understand."

"No, explain it. Because I hoop, like, I do this. You talking crazy right now."

"That's cap, Jojo. I, like, hoop everyday, I work out, I get my five hundred shots up daily. I've never once seen any of you in the gym outside of practice. It's cool, you guys have other interests, like your rapping and stuff. It's cool. Do you." Ashley says.

Jojo can tell she is trying to sound sincere. "Hold up, you think we're all pretenders? You sound like Coach P."

"I love Coach P. Ashley's voice trails off. "Anyway, he's been my trainer and always been in my corner. You guys might want to start listening to what he's telling you."

Jojo realizes Ashley might have just been coming to the games to support her trainer, Coach P. He thinks about it. In his mind, all Coach P ever did was hate on him and the team. Jojo starts to remember the things Coach P has been saying, his rules and his principles.

"Hello?" Ashley's voice interrupts his thoughts.

"I actually am a hooper," Jojo says.

"Yeah, well, it's kind of something you shouldn't have to say. It's something you do."

"Yeah. Well, we're hoopers, all of us, the whole Squad."

"That's not what I saw against Brampton. Talk is cheap."

"Okay, let's stop living in the past," Jojo says, trying to change the subject. "So you'll only date hoopers?"

"No, I mean, that's just one thing."

Jojo starts to realize how he can get closer to Ashley.

"And you'd still be number two." Ashley giggles.

"Who's number one?" Jojo hopes it's not Jason. But he really wants to know.

"Basketball, dummy," Ashley says, laughing.

"I'm number two. Ooh, I think she likes me!" Jojo sings, teasing.

"Oh my gosh, now who's talking crazy?" Ashley laughs. "I have to get some sleep, got an early workout at the community centre tomorrow morning. Bye, Jojo."

"Peace, peace," Jojo says.

As soon as Ashley hangs up, a plan forms in Jojo's mind. Not only is he going to show Coach Pritchard that he was wrong about him, but he is going to show Ashley, too.

Jojo knows he has to get the team on board to do it. He picks up his Xbox controller — all the players on the Squad are online.

"Yo, what up, Squad," Jojo says.

"What's up, Jojo? I was just killing Jose in 2K," Jazz says.

"Bruh, I was distracted," Jose says.

"With Liz, Jose?" Jojo asks.

"Chill, Jojo," Jose says.

"I didn't come on here to throw shade. Guys, I know how we can stick it to Coach P."

"Go on," Brendo says.

"Coach P thinks we're a bunch of pretend hoopers, right? We need to show him we're for real."

"How?"

"It's winter break. I say we train hard over the break. We get up five hundred shots a day and we work out everyday for the next two weeks. Then we ball out," Jojo says. If the routine works for Ashley, it will work for them.

"Okay, Jojo, the three Ps and ABCs, huh?" Ram says.

Jojo remembers Ashley's words about listening to what Coach P has been telling them. "Something like that, Ram. But against Coach, not for him."

"I'm feeling this," Brendo says.

"We come back in shape, skills on point. And we just start killing teams, right in Coach's face," Jojo says.

"I'd love to see the look on his face," Ram says.

"Word. It will shut him right up," Jazz says.

"So, y'all down?" Jojo asks.

"All the way," Brendo says.

"In for a penny . . . " Jose says.

"Aight, bet. Let's meet at the community centre early tomorrow morning," Jojo says.

15 GRINDING

Early in the morning, as promised, the team shows up at the community centre to train with Jojo. Just as Jojo hoped, Ashley is there. But it looks like she has been there for hours. She's drenched with sweat.

Jojo walks up to her as she works on her ball handling.

"What are you guys doing here?" Ashley asks.

"We about to get that work in," Jojo says. "You know, hooper stuff."

Ashley smiles. "Really? Okay, count me in."

"Didn't you just work out?" Jojo asks.

"Ballers ball," Ashley says.

Jojo shrugs his shoulders. Next to Ashley, he feels like a pretender.

For the rest of that morning, the boys go through all the drills Coach Pritchard made them do in practice. Everyone is working as hard as they can. Ashley does the drills with the boys. She is so good at them that it makes the rest of the boys try even harder just to keep up.

Grinding

After two gruelling hours, another group comes in with badminton rackets. The community centre clerk, a lean woman with short black hair and dark rimmed glasses, storms into the gym. "Okay! Open gym is over, people! Like, ten minutes ago. Now leave!" she shrieks. She gives Ashley a stink-face look.

Ashley kisses her teeth. "Can't stand her. Always kicking me out," Ashley whispers.

"Yo, chill, Ash," Jojo says. "Damn, she just doing her job." Ashley takes her basketball more seriously than Jojo has ever seen.

The boys give each other daps and start to pack up.

Jojo stands beside Ashley as she gathers her gear. "Good workout," he says.

"Yeah, you too. Y'all coming back tomorrow? Or are you one and done for the break?" Ashley asks.

"One and done? Nah, we'll be here," Jojo says.

"See ya later." Ashley touches Jojo's arm and walks out.

That touch makes Jojo feel about ten feet tall.

Brendo walks over, smiling from ear to ear.

"What are you so happy about?" Jojo asks.

"Kim texted me," Brendo says. "We're back together."

"Good, maybe now you can stop crying," Jojo says. "Jose, why didn't you tell anyone about you and Liz?"

"I don't kiss and tell, bro," Jose says.

"Yeah, right. She told you not to tell anyone, didn't she?" Jojo says.

Jose smiles.

"Same time tomorrow, Jo." Jazz shouts.

"Yeah, gang. You already know," Jojo shouts.

Jojo is feeling good about his plan. It's working. He can tell things between him and Ashley are changing for the better. And the team seems to be getting closer too. He's never been this friendly with Jazz.

For the next two weeks, the boys train and work out together. They shoot hundreds of shots each day and run suicides for conditioning. Ashley being there actually helps push the boys. She is so intense, skilled and in shape that it pushes the boys to work extra hard just to keep up with her. With everything to prove, Jojo leads the way.

As Jojo and Ashley grow closer, the team starts to hit their stride. They are running faster, looking stronger and making more shots.

Jojo notices that he isn't feeling the burning sensation in his chest when he runs a lot. It actually feels good. He notices that his shot is going in more consistently. And his game with Ashley is improving too.

"See you later," Ashley says to Jojo as she leaves the gym.

"Fo sho," Jojo gives a head nod and smiles.

For the first time, Jojo can't wait to get back in front of Coach Pritchard. He wants show the coach just how wrong he was about the team, and especially about him. He imagines Coach P apologizing to the whole team for thinking they were quitters and pretenders. The thought of Coach P having to eat his words fills Jojo with joy.

***

The rematch between the Squad and the Brampton Bulldogs is one of the most anticipated games of the year. Brampton is hosting and their crowd is the rowdiest. Jojo knows there is bad blood between the two teams, bad blood that Jojo started. Now Jojo and the Squad have payback on their minds. He remembers how Brampton put a real whooping on the Squad on their own court. He remembers the dunk on Brendo and his own confrontation with Prince.

Jojo, Brendo and Jose exit the locker room and make their way to the gym. Suddenly, a throng of rowdy fanboys with royal-blue painted faces and bodies block their path.

"Ya'll are trash!" the Brampton fans shout.

"Hey, Jojo, how's Ashley?" one kid yells. He re-enacts his ankles getting broken, then high-fives his friend. Another kid has his phone out, playing the video of Ashley schooling Jojo. He holds the phone to Jojo's face.

Just then, Jazz runs out and smacks the phone out of the kid's hands. "Back off the mandem!" Jazz shouts. "Let's get this!"

The Squad sprints onto the court to begin warm-up. As soon as they hit the court, the crowd starts booing.

Westwood has bussed in its own section filled with students and parents to cheer on the Squad. Looking into the stands, Jojo sees that half of the entire Brampton student body is at the game, and the gym is rocking. The Brampton team takes the court and the crowd goes nuts.

Jojo searches the crowd and spots Ashley. He reminds himself, *no distractions,* and shifts his focus to his teammates. Out of the corner of his eye, he sees Coach Pritchard watching him from the sideline.

"Hey, bring it in," Jojo calls the team in to a huddle.

"Yo, these guys are ranked," Brendo says. "We beat them, we get that wildcard into the playoffs, baby."

"Say less," Jose says.

"Forget Brampton, this game is bigger than them. We been grinding because of that freaking guy!" Jojo points to Coach P. "Let's show him and everyone else that we some real ones. *Screw Coach* on three."

The boys cheer, the gym is so loud their cheer is drowned out by screaming teenagers. Jojo, Jose and Brendo start their intro routine. Today their dance moves are extra hype.

"You better play as hard as y'all dance," Coach Pritchard says as the boys cut up.

16 Swagger LIKE US

From the opening tipoff, the game is a back-and-forth battle. The Squad is battling hard, running its offense and competing on every play. But charged up by the home crowd, Prince Bol comes out on fire, making tough shots. The Bulldogs take a quick eight-point lead over the Squad.

"Chill!" Jojo yells to his teammates. Jojo looks to the sideline and sees Coach Pritchard, who's surprisingly calm and quiet. He calmly motions to the referee for a time out.

The boys come into the huddle, expecting to hear it from their coach. Instead, Coach squats down in front of them, calmly pulls out his game board and draws up a press break.

"They're going to press you all game," he says. "You beat a pressing team by handling the pressure and staying in attack mode. Jojo, when you get the ball in the middle, just go."

Jojo is shocked. He looks at Coach Pritchard,

waiting for him to say something negative.

"Jojo, you got it?" Coach asks.

"Yes, Coach." Jojo says, wondering when Coach is going to let him have it.

"If they collapse, you got kick outs to Jose or Jazz for threes."

"See me," Jose says.

"You already know," Jojo replies.

Coach adds, "and see Brendo and Ram cutting, you might have them too. Stay in attack mode. Got it?"

Jojo nods.

Using the press break, the Squad claw their way back into the game. Jojo is attacking the hoop and setting up his teammates for open shots. One after another, the shots fall. Everyone chips in.

Towards the end of the first quarter, Jojo has the ball in the middle of the court. As he races up the court, he sees Jose sprinting up the court on his left side.

"See me!" Jose shouts.

Jojo whips a bullet pass to Jose. Jose catches the ball and lets the three-pointer fly from the corner.

Swack! The ball splashes through the net.

BZZZ! The scoreboard emits a loud buzzing sound to end the first half. The score is tied at 28–28.

"What!" Jose shouts as he skips up the court.

Jojo chest bumps him. "That's what I'm talking about," Jojo says.

★★★

At halftime, in the locker room, the mood is high energy. But Jojo feels like Coach is acting even more strange. Coach walks into the locker room and stands there, looking at his board.

The silence is awkward. But Coach has nothing to say.

Jojo begins to swell up with excitement. It's working. He looks at Brendo and Jose, and makes eye contact with the other players. All of them can sense it.

"Keep it going," Coach says, and walks out.

The boys look at each other, smirks creeping across their faces.

"You see his face?" Brendo asks.

"Let's stay focused," Jojo says.

In the third quarter, Keyshawn goes off. He scores six straight points. On his last bucket, he drives the ball baseline right past Brendo and then dunks with a one-handed leaner.

The Brampton crowd erupts, cheering loudly and getting crazy.

"They dun know! Me a Rude boy, bad man!" Keyshawn shouts.

Prince bumps Brendo as he runs back. "Mandem trash," Prince says.

On three straight possessions, Jojo answers back. He scores six points by making three consecutive mid-range jumpers. Then he puts his finger to his lips, telling the crowd to be quiet.

The games goes back and forth. Midway through the fourth quarter, Brendo comes alive. Jojo can see that Brendo is feeling bouncy. He soars high above the rim and snatches an offensive rebound. He lays it back into the hoop and then slaps the glass hard. Then he steals a pass and makes an acrobatic, double clutch layup over Prince.

With two minutes left, the Squad is up by six points. Sensing victory is close, the boys stop attacking and try to run out the clock. Big mistake. Brampton claws their way back and ties it with thirty seconds left.

"One stop," Jojo shouts.

Prince has the ball, with Brendo guarding him. Jojo stands in the paint, ready to help.

Prince crosses Brendo with a wicked crossover and drives it to the hoop. Brendo recovers and stays on Prince's hip. Prince leaps and Brendo jumps with him. Brendo soars high in the air and stuffs Prince's shot with two hands. Brendo's momentum sends him crashing into the end wall. The ball bounces right into Prince's hands, and he's right under the rim. He is about to lay the ball in for the easy two points when Jojo comes sprinting in.

Jojo leaps as high as he can.

"Give me that!" he says, as he pins the ball against the glass, then secures it.

Jojo takes off. The crowd is so loud that he doesn't hear his teammates shouting at him to stop. Jojo races down the court. A Brampton player lunges at him and he nearly loses the ball, but he gets it back. He dribbles to the hoop, but two Brampton players head him off at the rim. Prince, in full pursuit, is just a few feet behind Jojo as he enters the painted area. Prince is bearing down on him. Jojo sneaks a quick peek behind him and sees that Brendo is joining the play. Brendo is sprinting in behind Prince and pointing at the rim.

Jojo leaps towards the rim. Prince jumps after him. Jojo floats the ball backwards over Prince's fingers. Soaring above Prince, Brendo catches the ball above Prince's head. Prince falls face forward. Brendo grips Prince's forehead as he slams the ball through the rim.

The Westwood section of the crowd goes crazy. Brendo is screaming and flexing. Then he steps over Prince where he's lying on the ground.

All the players know there is a list of things you can do on a basketball court that are universally seen as downright disrespectful. Stepping over your opponent after you have dunked all over them is at the top of the list.

Prince kicks at Brendo, catching him in the calf, as he walks away. The referee grabs Brendo before he can react.

Tweet!

The referee hits Prince with a double technical

foul and tosses him out of the game for being unsportsmanlike.

The students and some parents in the Brampton crowd throw debris onto the court. The crowd is hostile. The school principal stands up at the scorer's table to reprimand the students over the microphone.

As the referee escorts him off the court, Prince turns towards Brendo. "Watch your back," Prince says.

"Scoreboard!" Jojo yells at the crowd as the clock runs out.

In the locker room, Jojo checks his phone. He has thousands of new followers. The video of Brendo's dunk has gone viral and they are calling him "Boom" on the internet.

There is no post-game talk from Coach Pritchard. He lets the team celebrate.

"Whew!" Brendo shouts, putting his arm around Jojo.

Jojo continues getting changed.

"What's your hurry?" Brendo asks.

"Ashley's team is playing right now," Jojo says.

"Now who's in love?"

"*Pshht*," Jojo says awkwardly. He bolts out of the locker room.

By the time Jojo reaches the gym, the crowd is already in a frenzy.

"That girl is dope," Jojo hears someone in the crowd say.

Jojo checks the score. The girls' Squad are already

up eight points and it hasn't been two minutes into the game.

Ashley gets the ball and the crowd rises to their feet. Jojo looks around in bewilderment. She dribbles up the court and spins around her defender. She hits the next defender with an in-and-out dribble and then a crossover. She hesitates, freezing another defender, then uses a pound dribble and a sidestep to get her jumper off.

Swack! Nothing but net. She raises three slender fingers in the air, then flicks them subtly. Jojo realizes she's waving at the crowd, and anyone else who wants some, to bring it.

"She's nice, nice." Jojo whispers.

It's one of the nicest moves Jojo has ever seen anyone do, she is electric. Even more shocking to Jojo, Ashley doesn't celebrate. Instead, she gets right into the face of the other team's point guard. Her pressure knocks the player off balance as the inbound comes.

Ashley intercepts the pass, she dribbles the ball behind the arc. Without hesitation, she launches a fadeaway three, kicking her leg out like she's Kobe.

Swish!

"Merk, Ashley, Merk!" Jojo shouts like a fanboy.

17 Preparation MEETS OPPORTUNITY

Jojo paces back and forth in the locker room. He's never felt so nervous. He feels like there are butterflies in his stomach and cobwebs in his head. The other boys look focused and seriously dialled into the task at hand. Jojo starts to worry. What if he lets everyone down? Jojo does his best to shake that negative thought from his mind, but still it lingers. What if?

Jojo takes a seat as Coach Pritchard bursts through the locker room doors. Coach's demeanour is as cool as a fan. "Everyone's here on time, stretched out and ready to go. Three Ps, check. I already know you're going to bring that same ABC energy you brought yesterday. Just remember that last P, no matter what happens out there, persevere. I know you will. Okay, come out when you're ready."

Coach pats Jojo on the shoulder and whispers, "just believe."

The negative thoughts in Jojo's head crumble. Instead of thinking *what if I don't?* Jojo starts to think *what if I do?*

The boys look at each other, confused and puzzled at Coach's words.

Jojo sits there, silent. In his mind he can hear all the things that Coach has been yelling at him and the team. He remembers how Coach wanted him to be a leader and how he told him that there was no one stopping him but him.

"I got it all wrong," Jojo says quietly.

The team nods their heads. Jojo can see the realization on their faces.

"Did we just get Jedi mind tricked by Coach P?" Jose asks.

"He played us," Ram says, nodding.

"Nah, we were playing ourselves. Guys, that's on me," Jojo says, standing up. "Coach P was crazy tough on us, me especially, and I got in my feelings. But now I know why he did it. Remember? He said that if we worked hard enough we'd have a chance to do something special, and here we are!"

"He's right." Jazz says.

"Well, we here now! We up in this now Squad!"

"Say less, bro," Jose says.

"Let's go!"

The boys cheer and charge out of the locker room to face their opponents, the Scarborough Raiders.

On the opening tipoff, Kofi, the Raiders' centre, a large African with a baby fro, intentionally elbows Jojo in the mouth. But the ref doesn't see it.

"Ref!" Jojo yells as blood wells in his mouth.

"I didn't see it," the ref shouts.

Coach Pritchard runs onto the court to call time out.

Tweet!

"What do you mean you didn't see that!" Coach shouts at the ref. "You better watch what's going on here!"

Coach runs up to Jojo and sneakily slips him a towel. Jojo spits into it.

"Don't let them see you bleed, son. Give me that." Coach snatches the towel and then places his arm around Jojo. "You took a shot. You good? Check if you have all your teeth."

Jojo smiles. He realizes that Coach P really has his back. And everything Coach P made him do has only made him stronger and a better basketball player.

From that point on, Jojo gives extra effort on every play, holding nothing back. The game becomes very physical, and the ref lets most of it go.

Late in the fourth quarter, with the score 63–60 for the Raiders, Jojo jostles for position in the post against Kofi. He gets low, throws his body into Kofi and wedges some space. He holds his seal as Jose passes the ball into him.

"You got nuttin," Kofi snorts.

"Hold this," Jojo says.

Jojo sees Brendo cutting. He slips a neat pocket pass to Brendo. But before Brendo can lay it in, his defender pushes him. Heading out of bounds, Brendo flips the ball back to Jojo.

Brendo lands awkwardly and rolls his ankle. "Arrgh!" Brendo shouts, clutching his ankle.

Jojo caught the ball and didn't hesitate, he pulled up for the jumpshot over Kofi's hand.

Swack! The ball splashes through the net.

"Bro, you can't guard me," Jojo shouts as he and Jose rush over to help Brendo.

Brendo can barely walk. He limps off the court.

Jojo looks up at the scoreboard. He's brought them within a point, the score is 63–62 with just over forty seconds left to play. On the bench, Brendo has his head bowed and covered with a towel, his leg spread out on the bench. Coach P is taping his ankle. Jojo's heart drops as Harmon runs clumsily to the scorer's table to check in.

"You need one stop. Stay connected!" Coach P shouts from the edge of the bench.

"We got you, Coach," Jojo says.

The Raiders run the clock down to fifteen seconds and then throw it into Kofi in the post. Jojo gets ready to stop his shot. Kofi backs him down. As soon as Kofi turns to shoot, Jojo leaps into the air to block it. But Kofi fakes the shot, and now, with Jojo out of position, he has a wide open layup to win the game.

Suddenly, Jose comes sprinting through the paint. He leaps and swats the ball out of Kofi's hands. The seconds tick down as the ball bounces off some hands and rolls towards the sideline.

Harmon gives chase. Jojo has never seen Harmon run that fast and smoothly. Harmon dives and knocks the ball off a Raiders' defender and out of bounds.

"Yes!" Jojo and the Squad boys run over and help Harmon back to his feet.

"Yeah, Jose!"

"Not in my house!" Jose shouts.

"Yeah, Harmon!" the boys shout as they run back to their bench.

Coach P is jumping up and down and yelling at the ref about something to do with the shot clock.

"Sorry, Coach." The referee shrugs his shoulders.

With just three seconds left in the game, with the Squad down by one point, Coach P calls his final time out.

When the boys get to the bench, Coach P already has the play drawn up. He squats down in front of them and taps his board. "This is how we win the game." He looks straight at Jojo. "Start here, right in front of the ball. Ask for it, and I mean yell like you want it bad. Harmon, you run up and set this back screen on Kofi, and I mean set it hard. Jose, you throw the lob to Jojo, and that's game. Got it?"

The boys clap and cheer.

Jojo takes a deep breath. All game he's been locked in. But now he can feel his attention waver. He scans the stands, looking for Ashley.

Coach Pritchard puts a firm hand on his shoulder. Instantly, Jojo refocuses on the game. Coach P taps Jojo in the chest and smiles a big toothy grin. "Just believe," Coach P says.

The Squad set up the play.

The referee hands Jose the ball.

"Here! Here!" Jojo yells. Kofi shifts his position to deny him the ball. Harmon runs up and sets the hard back screen on Jojo's man. Jojo spins and takes off, running towards the basket.

Jose throws the ball high up into the air, towards the hoop. But Jojo can tell the ball has been overthrown. If he can catch it, he isn't sure how he is going to shoot it. Jojo takes two more big steps and leaps into the air. Kofi comes charging over and leaps, momentarily blinding Jojo of the path of the ball.

Arms fully outstretched, Jojo catches the ball in his fingertips. The catch is so difficult he has no chance to shoot it in mid-air. Jojo comes back down with the ball and desperately flicks it up over his head in the direction of the hoop. He hasn't actually seen the hoop.

The buzzer sounds as Jojo regains his balance, but the gym is dead silent.

Jojo looks at the hoop. He sees the ball teetering on the rim. The balls spins around once. And then bounces off the backboard. And then bounces off the front rim. And then, slowly, drops through the net.

A deafening roar explodes from the crowd.

Jojo triumphantly puts his hands in the air and drops to his knees. The last thing he sees before his teammates pile on top of him is Coach P pointing at him.

Jojo reads his lips. Coach is yelling, "I told you."

"Let's go!" Jojo shouts.

18 BLOWOUT

Jojo sits at his locker. He feels so amazing, it almost doesn't seem real. In the last game, he hit the biggest shot of his life and he has no idea how or why it happened. But it did.

Jojo thinks about all the team has been through with Coach P. And despite it all, here they are, just one win away from the provincials.

Coach P walks into the locker room and places his hand on Jojo's shoulder. "Luck favours the prepared man," he says.

"Yes, Coach," Jojo says.

"Settle down, boys," Coach says to the team. "There's more work to do, and our next opponent, those boys from Carson Academy in Toronto, are no joke."

The locker room quiets down. The boys take their seats.

Carson Academy is the top ranked team in Toronto. They are undefeated and they are tough as nails. Jojo has been following some of their players on the 'Gram, and they look like they are legit hoopers.

As Coach reviews Carson's roster, he circles two names on the whiteboard. "Mafooz and AC are two D1 hoopers. We have to contain them and be ready to help our teammates on them at all times. Brendo, you have AC. Jojo, you're going to start on Mafooz."

Brendo winces and massages his ankle.

"Suck it up, bro," Jojo whispers to Brendo. Brendo nods.

Jojo takes a deep breath. Mafooz is considered one of the best players in the entire province. Jojo has seen his highlights and, as far as he can tell, Mafooz has no weaknesses.

"Win this and you're in the provincials," the Coach goes on. "But you'll need to leave it all on the floor tonight and go to war."

Jose stands up and starts banging rhythmically on the locker. Jojo looks around. All the boys are nodding their heads to the beat.

Jojo stands up and starts singing like he's the artist Rasheeda. "We ready, we ready, we reaaaaady for war."

The rest of the team joins in.

"We ready, we ready!"

"What! What! What!" Jazz and Ram shout.

"We reeeady, for war!" the team continues.

Coach nods his head to the beat. It's the first time they've ever seen Coach P get hype.

"Let's go!" Coach shouts and charges out of the locker room.

During warm-up, the entire team is hype. The Squad jump up and down in a circle, cheering, their arms locked on each other's shoulders.

Roar! The Carson supporters in the crowd erupt as Carson takes the floor.

Watching Carson warm up in their cool black and gold uniforms, Jojo and the Squad start to lose their nerve. Every Carson player is as tall as Jojo, and it's a spectacular dunk after dunk in their warm-up line.

Jojo hears the crowd gasp. He sees Mafooz take off and do a 360, tomahawk dunk.

"Oh, my god," Jose says.

Jojo looks back at Coach Pritchard, who is pointing at Jojo to gather the team together.

"Yo, bring it in, guys," Jojo calls. Jojo can feel that the Carson team has taken their energy just from warming up.

"We ain't scared!" Jojo shouts. "All the pressure is on them. We ain't scared. Let's knuckle up! Squad up!"

Jojo looks up into the stands. The gym is packed — it's standing room only. Jojo spots Ashley. Earlier, her team won and advanced to the provincials. She's still wearing her jersey. She looks straight at Jojo and holds her fist up.

Ashley is so hardcore, Jojo thinks to himself. For a moment, he thinks he might be in love with her.

Focus. Jojo catches himself.

Jojo lines up to take the tipoff against Mafooz. Jojo sizes him up. Mafooz has muscles popping out everywhere on his body.

Mafooz stares down Jojo without blinking, but doesn't say a word and doesn't break eye contact. Jojo looks away, but he can tell Mafooz is still staring at him.

AC, a white, lanky, long-limbed guard, wears a headband that looks like a shoelace. He and Brendo jostle for position.

The ref throws the ball up. Before Jojo can jump, Mafooz launches himself high in the sky and tips the ball ahead to a teammate. Then he takes off running. Jojo realizes Mafooz is moving faster than he can think. He tries to catch up, but Mafooz is just too fast.

AC throws an alley-oop up to Mafooz. All Jojo can do is watch as Mafooz two-hand spikes it through the rim. Mafooz comes off the rim with no expression. Jojo looks at his face and sees nothing but focus and coldness in his eyes.

That dunk rattles the Squad.

"Did you see how high he was?" Jose asks.

"The guy is a cyborg," Jojo says.

Carson puts the press on. The Squad tries to run their press break, but their passes keep getting deflected and stolen. First AC steals it and hits a step-back three-pointer right in Brendo's face. Then another steal by

Carson on the inbound. And then another, and then another. All steals lead to baskets.

The last basket comes from Mafooz. He steals the ball and drives it along the baseline. He leaps and soars high above Jojo to drop the ball into the hoop. Jojo can just stand and watch. It's like Mafooz is wearing a jetpack. The squad is on the verge of being blown out.

Brendo starts limping.

"Don't start that."

"What?!"

Tweet!

Coach Pritchard runs out onto the floor in between Brendo and Jojo. "Time out!"

19 Deserve VICTORY

The Squad hasn't been able to cross half court and already the score is 11–0. They're rattled.

"No one is open," Jose yells.

"Set the damn screen," Brendo says as the boys return to the bench.

"I tried," Jazz says. "He's too fast."

"Chill with all that *too fast* stuff. We just need to man up." Jojo tries to calm his teammates.

Jojo knows it, there is no denying it — Carson is for real. The way they move and the speed of their cuts is intense. Jojo knows no one on the team has played against players of this skill level. It seems like everyone in the gym knows it. Even the Westwood supporters in the crowd have gone quiet.

"Fake your passes before you make them. Everyone needs to —" Coach pauses. Suddenly his face turns intense. "You can't back down from these guys! If you want to beat them you have to fight back! Handle the pressure. Be ball tough. Keep your heads in it.

Stick together. Come on now, fight back!" Coach P encourages.

The boys take the floor with renewed energy.

Jojo catches the ball in the middle of the floor and drives it hard to the hoop. He powers through the defense and forces up the only type of shot he knows.

Mafooz soars by him and slaps his shot into the stands. "Hell naw," Mafooz says in a Nigerian accent.

In the very next play, Jojo catches the ball. He drives it to the hoop. The Carson defense collapses again, but this time, Jojo passes it out to Jazz. Jazz rises up and knocks down the three-pointer. It's their first points of the half, but it seems to energize the squad.

On the next play, AC skips down the court and drops a no-look pass to Mafooz. Jojo sees the play and steps in front of Mafooz. He jumps as high as he can. Jojo stuffs Mafooz before he can take off.

"Give me that!" Jojo yells.

"That's the fight!" Coach P yells.

Mafooz smirks.

Suddenly, Jose comes alive. He makes a hissing sound as he reaches for the ball.

Jojo passes it to Jose, he catches it on the move, dekes a defender and then dribbles into a deep three.

Splash! Through the net.

"Let's go!" Jose shouts.

Jojo can feel the energy from his teammates, like nothing he's ever experienced before. The Squad fight their way back into the game with hustle and scrappy play.

Jojo dives on the floor for a loose ball. He fires the ball ahead to Brendo, then hustles to join the play. Brendo fires it back to Jojo just as he crosses half. Jojo takes two more dribbles, eyes the hoop and pulls up from just inside of half court, from the Carson Academy logo.

The crowd gasps.

Swack! The ball splashes through the net.

Jojo screams, "I do this!" at the top of his lungs.

Right away, AC gets the ball, dribbles down and pulls up for three from the exact same spot.

Swack! AC jogs back, holding his follow-through, staring at Jojo.

"It's like that? Here!" Jose gives Jojo the ball.

Time is ticking down in the second quarter as Jojo dribbles the ball up the court. Mafooz is hounding him.

Brendo sets a hard screen on Mafooz, as AC switches to guard Jojo. Jojo glances up at the scoreboard. Three seconds left. Jojo dribbles hard like he's going to the hoop, and then steps back behind the three-point line.

Three, two, one — AC recovers and jumps to challenge the shot. Jojo lets the shot go.

"Water!" Jojo shouts.

Splash! Nothing but net.

At halftime, Jojo encourages his team, "We got this!"

The Squad has clawed their way back into it but still trail Carson 30–23.

In the second half, Carson is a different team. They start trapping all over the court. Jojo feels like he's always playing against two defenders, and the Squad's offense grinds to a halt.

Carson starts to light it up. First Mafooz hits a sidestep three, then AC hits a pull up three from deep. Then Mafooz steals the inbound pass, he throws the ball off the backboard and reverse dunks it.

Frustrated, the Squad players start blaming each other.

"Make better passes!" Brendo shouts.

"Play some defense!" Jose says.

"Stop hiding," Jazz says.

Jojo huddles them up. "Keep fighting. C'mon now, stay together," Jojo says.

Jojo and his teammates fight as hard as they can, but they can't cut into the lead. Carson cruises to victory. 60–34.

As the clock runs out on their season, Jojo can feel the tears well up in his eyes.

On the way to the locker room, tears stream down Jojo's face. Ashley meets him in the hallway. Jojo doesn't even bother trying to hide his tears, no more pretending.

Ashley hugs him. She pulls back and kisses him on the side of the cheek, catching part of his lips at the same time. "You did your best," she says.

Jojo nods. Despite his sorrow, it still registers that Ashley kissed him, even if it was because he's crying. He knows he won't soon forget the feeling of her cheek against his and her soft lips on his.

Brendo and Jose are devastated. Tears roll down their faces as they walk up and place their arms around Jojo.

"I'll call you later," Ashley says.

Jojo nods.

The whole team sits in the locker room, most of them crying. Coach Pritchard walks in. He stands in the middle of the room for a moment.

"Hey now, that's enough feeling sorry for ourselves. Clear your eyes and hold your heads up. You have nothing to be ashamed about!" Coach P shouts.

The boys pull themselves together. Jojo wipes his tears and composes himself.

Coach goes on. "You lost to a team that was better than you. There's no shame in that. But remember this pain. Remember all the grinding you did to get here. Understand that if you don't want to feel this pain again, then that grind, those three Ps, your ABCs must become a way of life. Then, and only then, will you deserve victory."

Jojo stands up and starts hugging each of his teammates. *Coach is right*, he thinks. They only grinded for a short while and for all the wrong reasons. Carson has been on their grind forever and it shows.

"Now huddle up," orders Jojo. The team gets up

and forms a circle around Coach. "Let's end this season right, two upsets ain't bad for an unranked Squad. Clap for Coach!" Jojo says.

The boys start clapping for their coach, but to their surprise, he starts to woo dance.

"What!" Jojo can't believe what they're seeing.

"Aye, aye, aye, aye, yah! Aye, aye, aye, aye, yah!" The boys shout as Coach is turned up and woo walks.

Jojo and the rest of the boys join in the woo dance, legs popping everywhere. "Aye, yah!" Jojo and the rest of the boys shout as they leap into the air with their coach.

"Okay, okay, y'all didn't know Coach had it like that, huh? Oh, and Jojo," Coach says. "I'm proud of you for stepping up and leading this team. I hope you now see what I saw in you all along. I'm expecting big things from you next year."

"Yes, Coach," Jojo says.

"And I see you playing kissy face with Ashley Vasquez. Oh, and cute love note, too." Coach P says with a big smile.

Jojo's jaw drops. Coach laughs heartily.

"I'm proud of you boys," Coach says again, and walks out of the locker room.

The team breaks into laughter.

"You should have seen your face, Jo," Jose says. "Coach put you on blast."

Jojo shakes his head.

"Coach P, man. This guy is always cheesing me!"